Petals of Blue

PART 1

WILTED DUET

Y.V. LARSON

Cover Design – Lune Aesthete
Editor – Scarlett Chase from Scarlett Pen Edits
Proof Reader - Erica C.
Alpha Readers – Angelica Heitbrink, Patricia Conway, Brandi
Augustine, Kassandra Melendez
Character Art - ART by ALEKSA

✾ Formatted with Vellum

Trigger Warning

Please read the following list if you have any triggers. Note that these could be considered spoilers!

If you have any questions or believe I missed a trigger warning, you may reach out to me through social media, or via email: Author@yvlarson.com

- Kidnapping
- PTSD responses
- Flashbacks
- Injuries
- Harassment
- Mental health struggles
- Violence
- Alcohol and drug use
- Mentions of bullying
- Mentions of childhood abuse (sexual, physical, and emotional) and neglect
- Mentions of parental death

This is a slow-burn MMFMM why-choose romance, meaning two men are also in a sexual/romantic/loving relationship. Part one ends on a steep cliffhanger.

Prologue

ERICA

There are moments that break you. Bits of time that shatter your perception of the future. Some that change you fundamentally and steal your hope.

For me, those punches came one right after another over the course of eight months. The hits of betrayal hurt so much I had no choice but to fortify my walls and harden my heart.

The pain wasn't the beginning, but that's what made it worse. Friendship and loyalty were the start of our story. The five of us were inseparable during high school. Until I had to move. What once was camaraderie and young love turned into silent heartbreak. The boys who brightened my days cut me out of their lives and cast a shadow over my future.

Without them, in a scary home of uncertainty and hostility, Erica became Blue.

Here shows the slow death of Erica Bennett.

Text Threads

Texting...

DECLAN 🧡

Me: We made it safe. Already mad about the tiny room.

Read

Me: Missing you already! Will you come visit me soon?

Read

Me: Declan... You okay?

Read

Me: Are you mad at me??

Read

Me: It's been a month Dec. Seriously, what's wrong?

Read

Declan 🧡: Leave me alone, Erica. Move on.

Declan was the first to befriend me. How could he also be the first to break me? Life had a funny way of tearing me down. My hope of him responding held me in a chokehold for too many long weeks. Until he got sick of me and shattered the only support and source of love I had.

One hour wasn't supposed to separate us. They had cars and their licenses, plus...they *promised*. So...*why*?

I don't think I'll ever know why he ghosted me, but one thing's for certain: Declan Ledger, my best friend and crush, abandoned me.

Texting...
ROMAN

> Me: Safe, no need to worry anymore!
> Although, this house is a dump

Read

> Me: You and Dec doing something?
> Haven't heard from either of you.

Read

> Me: I'm getting worried.

Read

> Me: Did I do something wrong?

Read

Me: It's been two months since your brother told me to leave him alone. I guess I'll assume that extends to you. Good bye.

Read

I never did hear back from Roman. Declan's older brother was always around, and I secretly had a crush on him since they moved to my high school. I'm sure he saw me as a younger sister who tagged along with all the boys, but he was more than that to me. Then he became another Ledger who wounded my already bleeding heart.

Texting...

JARED 💙

Me: Miss you. Please send help, lol.

Read

Me: The Ledger brothers are ignoring me. What's up?

Read

Me: I just tried to call you. Aunt Linda's boyfriend punched a hole in the wall tonight. I could use someone to talk to.

Read

Me: J...

That one hurt the most. Jared had my soul in the palm of his hand with his bubbly smile and outgoing personality. He was my match in every way, and yet he dropped me the moment I was forced to move a few hours away.

Whatever happened, they were in on it together. And why wouldn't they be? Jared and Declan were best friends from the moment I introduced them in our freshman year.

Texting...

FELIX

Me: Hey!

Read

Me: Look, I know we weren't as close like the others, but I really need your help.

Read

Felix 🧡: If this is about the other three, don't bother.

Me: It's Aunt Linda's new boyfriend, asshole.

Read

Felix 🧡: Can't help you, babe. You know how to throw a punch. Peace out.

Me: What the fuck, Felix?! He pushed me and I swear my door rattles at night. What if he gets in?!

Sent as text message.

That was the final nail in the coffin. Erica Bennett died eight months after moving from Seattle to Tacoma, Washington, but her story didn't end there.

The happy, lovable girl I used to be ceased to exist the night her aunt's boyfriend dislocated her shoulder, and she had nobody to turn to.

For eight months, Erica lost her sunshine. Then it returned in the form of a sad, blonde little girl.

At eighteen years old, Erica became Blue. Blue may have been depressed and terrified, but she fought to survive, even if it was only for Violet, the girl now in her care.

One

BLUE

"Blue, babe! Come take a shot with us!"

Shit. I strut my ass around him for the sake of tips, flirt a little to keep his college buddies coming back, and this is what I get. "Awww, sorry, Dale. I have a mess to clean up." *Lie. Christ, I hate working the floor.*

"Boo!" The blond, curly-haired guy pouts, but he's soon distracted by Bethany breezing past. My bestie is fucking stunning and far too sweet for these young frat boys. Especially not the one drooling over her; they look like they could be siblings.

"You're too sexy to clean shit, babe." Dale leans in, the stench of vodka making me just as nauseous as his pet name for me. "Have a drink with me."

Classic fucking asshole. Whatever happened to people saying please? And what makes this douche canoe think I'd trip over my high heels to hang out with him? I bet he's at least five years my junior.

"Maybe some other time, Dale," I say, adding a slight

rasp to my voice to keep him hooked. He may be an entitled jackass, but he gives good tips. And good tips mean another girls' night out. Or brunch. Ooo, or pizza.

"Blue!" my other bestie shouts.

With a girly wave, I leave Dale's table and hustle—elegantly—back behind the safety bar and sidle up to Janine. "'Sup?"

She glances at me with a frown while cracking the top of another beer. "What? Oh, I figured you could use a rescue."

I kiss her bare shoulder in appreciation. "Thanks, love."

Janine hums, her short black hair sticking to her neck as she powers through a lineup of Vodka Sevens.

"Screw that guy," Bethany huffs, coming up behind us to take a sip of water. "His friends are creeps."

I nod, laughing at her shiver of disgust. Both of us kick off our heels and slip our tennis shoes on so we can get back to helping Janine. Thankfully, the three of us can stay behind the bar now that a few waitresses are off their breaks.

We quickly fall into our usual rhythm mixing drinks, ignoring sexual innuendos, and generally making it through another busy night at Serpent's Kiss.

A very familiar beat roars through the club, drawing a grin from me and my girls. "Shots" by LMFAO draws the crowd to us, giving me the boost I need. Bopping my head and jumping up with Janine and Bethany between pouring shots is the vibe I fucking live for.

Sneaking a lemon drop with my besties, I tilt my

head back and let the thump of the bass flow through my body.

"SHOTS!" the crowd screams, making me grin. The people I serve may be incredibly handsy, judgmental, rude and a ton of other shit at times, but they're the definition of fun. And fun is what I live for these days.

With a big ass grin, I turn on my heel with a bottle of tequila in my grip. "Raise your hands if you're fucked up!" I bellow and relish the excitement I receive in return.

God, it feels good to help the people of Chicago have a good time. For the time being, I lose myself in their smiles and happiness. This line of work makes it easy for me to get lost in my head as I move through the motions. Instead of losing myself in my dark thoughts, I flirt, dance, and smile my heart out.

As the night winds down and partiers are stumbling out the door with security on their asses, my shoulders begin to slump.

"You okay?"

Glancing up from the now spotless counter, I find Kevin watching me worriedly. "Hey." I smile. Kevin's a great guy, and one of my best friends. "I'm good. You leaving?"

He glares at me, his dark eyes pinning me in place. "Not until you do, Blue. You know that."

I roll my eyes and finish my closing tasks. It's nice to have someone looking out for me, especially at three in the morning. "Thanks, bubs," I say to Kevin as he locks the door behind us.

He grumbles at the nickname, making me laugh. I'm

appreciative of how he escorts me to my car every night he can. "Drive safe, Blue. See you tomorrow."

"See ya."

My feet scream once I'm sitting, and I glare at the heels I toss in the back. I'm ready to sleep for *at least* twelve hours. Unless Violet wakes up early. Please let tomorrow morning be the day she actually sleeps in.

I turn the car key and dread the five-minute drive to my apartment, but I have to do it.

Sleep. I need sleep.

Two

BLUE

I feel fucking awful. Like death warmed up, and my neck is one wrong move away from pinching.

"Your poor hair! Why does it look like that?!" Dakota, my third wonderful friend and hair stylist, is staring at my messy, sweat-slicked braids like they're dying puppies.

Janine snorts into her coffee. Her black hair is in a cute low ponytail with a goddamn bow. Bitch looks like she didn't fucking close down the club with me last night.

Bethany frowns and nudges Dakota. "That's like telling another girl she looks awful."

"Thanks, Beth," I say dryly and take a big pull from my water bottle. "I went to class this morning and guess who didn't show up? You three!"

"Why the hell would I want to sweat my ass off on a bike at seven in the morning after closing last night?" Janine has a point, but I'm still pissy about it. At least our cycling instructor is amazing and kept me hyped up.

Although all that hype sputtered out as soon as I climbed off the death machine. It's been half an hour and I'm still regretting this morning's workout.

"Why in the world did you go to cycling class if you closed last night?" Dakota, with her perfect long dirty blonde waves, looks shocked and disgusted by my choices.

Groaning, I push my pastry aside and rub my eyes. "Dave has had me on closing shift every single night for the past month."

"Ever since you turned him down," Janine adds, like I need the fucking reminder that our bar manager is a sleazy asshole. "He's throwing a tantrum. It will pass."

Easy for her to say, but I keep my annoyance targeted toward the one who deserves it. "He's a prick. Anyway, if I didn't go to class after closing nights, I'd never go. Then what would happen?"

"You'd lose that fine ass you've worked so hard for," Dakota answers, sounding sad for me.

"Exactly." It sounds super shallow, but I'm confident with my body. It's the one thing I've always been able to control, so being fit has become incredibly important to me.

I'm not naturally curvy like Dakota, or model skinny like Bethany. This is one thing Janine and I have in common. Loving food—especially pizza and hash browns—with finicky metabolisms like ours means we have to work hard to have the physiques we want.

I still feel jealousy and awe over my friends' shapes,

and yet I like my own frame too. I don't know. Sometimes I love myself, sometimes I hate myself.

All I'm saying is I went cycling this morning so I could have a pastry for breakfast and pizza for dinner later without feeling bad about my yummy habits. It just really fucking sucks that I only got three hours of sleep.

Violet is the perfect, most exhausting alarm clock.

Dakota, probably sensing my thoughts like all hairstylists do, asks me about my girl. "How's V? Still a wrecking ball like her Ma?"

I groan. "Yes. I swear she always has a new adventure up her sleeve. Woke me up at six this morning for her next one."

In no way would I wish to change Violet. What I would *love* is an extra hour of sleep sometimes, but who wouldn't?

She keeps me busy, which helps my mind focus on the future and less on the past. There's so much back there, and when I allow it to weigh me down, I stumble. *Hard*. I can't afford to trip over my issues. That's been my motto since I was eighteen years old.

For eleven years, I've been burying my bullshit. That can't be healthy. The betrayals, hurts, and traumas have lived in their shallow graves since Violet came into my life.

She's my world. There's no fucking way I'm letting my past touch her.

Shoveling another metaphorical patch of dirt onto that reminder, I take a sip of my coffee. "So, where are we dancing this weekend?"

Just like that, lightness fills me as I discuss *my* next adventure with my besties. My life isn't about assholes and douchebags who leave me and bruise me. At least not anymore.

My life is all about food, snuggles with my girl, partying with my friends, shaking my ass, and making shit *better*.

That's all I would like to do—make my life better than it was.

I won't ever sink so deep again. Nothing will drag me down.

Three

BLUE

I lied. Nothing ruins my day faster than the horrible downward spiral of not knowing what to wear.

It always starts with not knowing, then goes to hating every piece of clothing I own, and ends with feeling hideous. I've worked hard for the wardrobe I have, and it's stupid that I can't figure out which sexy outfit I want to wear.

For years my closets were bare, and what I *did* have was threadbare and one puff of wind away from disintegrating.

All of my money and shopping were saved for Violet. Keeping her dressed, warm—especially through those Minnesota winters—and fitting in at school was my goal. I didn't care if I froze to death on the street walking home from another shift at the disgusting bar I worked at for way too long.

My aunt, on the other hand, didn't give two shits about me or V. That woman hardly looked twice at me since my parents died. God, I was just a kid when my mom and dad passed away.

For a long time, before Violet came along, the only hugs I got were from the guys—

My throat closes over with an emotion I'm well acquainted with. *What did I do to push them away? Why would they do that to me?*

Cursing, I throw my mascara back in its pouch because what's the fucking point if I'm just going to throw a pity party and probably cry myself to sleep like I've done so many times.

Again, *what is wrong with me?!* All these years later and I still get sucked into those assholes. The slightest inconvenience and I'm pondering all the ways I was unlikeable.

Honestly, I don't want to go out at this point. My room is a mess of outfits, and my skin fucking itches from all the fabrics.

Why is everything so unflattering tonight?!

In a thong and baggy T-shirt, I collapse onto my bed. "I'm not going." I snatch my phone and send that exact statement in the group chat. Bethany responds saying the same thing. Then Janine and Dakota are on our asses, deciding who's coming to me and who's going to Beth.

Apparently, they have just the thing to cheer us up. Cue my eye roll.

Vodka and a mini black dress were their bright ideas. I'm only slightly annoyed that it worked.

Just as I was about to fall asleep, Janine breezed through my bedroom door with a grin on her face. I made a note to talk to Violet about letting people into the apartment after nine at night.

That's a problem for tomorrow though because right now the drinks are flowing and the bass is thumping. Serpent's Kiss is absolutely feral tonight, and I'm so here for it.

We started at a different club, but nowhere else provides the hype of a dance floor like our place of work. Plus, we get discounts. We'd be dumb not to whoop it up here off duty.

Since Janine started me on vodka first, I've stuck to that. While I might have a night shift tomorrow and could sleep in, that's just not my life. Violet will probably rope me into something in the morning, and I'd rather not be fucked up on a bunch of different liquors.

I'm twenty-nine, so I know how to drink the right way. Dancing, on the other hand, not so much. Grinding and jumping around is all I've got. Bethany is sensual as hell tonight in her silver ruffles, though. She's such a kick ass dancer, it's no wonder everyone glances twice at her.

Since I'm trying not to be a piece of shit tomorrow,

I'm the most sober of the group. My job is to pay attention. So every time Beth is approached by wandering hands and lingering glances, I watch her cues. I'm hyperfocused on the scrunch of her nose and the cowering of her shoulders.

I weave and jump around her until the icky ones find their next target. While I love protecting my girls, Janine makes it a bit harder when she grinds on anything solid.

Her running rule is that we stop her if the guy or girl isn't her type. Janine's specific, so I'm always tugging her away and shaking my head. Every single time, she pouts, but once she gets a glance and sees that her dancing partner doesn't look exactly like the guy who broke her heart last year, she scowls and kisses my shoulder.

To anyone else, our show of appreciation might be strange, but it's our way of showing affection. I will love these women until my dying breath; you bet your ass we give each other kisses.

With all three of them solo and dancing within our mini group, I relax and let my head fall back on my shoulders. The music sounds like one loud noise, but I'm not in the sea of bodies for the lyrics. I'm here for the pounding of the bass and the sweaty bodies surrounding me.

It's a vibe that chases away the melancholy.

For now.

Heat scorches my tummy as a large hand splays across it. I suck in a gasp, shocked that I let someone sneak up on me. Beth, Janine, and Dakota are twirling around in a drunken circle, none the wiser to my predicament.

"Relax," an incredibly masculine voice rumbles in my ear. I stiffen for a moment, but when his hard body curls around me and the beat drops, I press my ass against his very hard cock.

The man groans, and I grin, getting lost in the feel of letting loose. If it were my night to go wild and not babysit my friends, I'd for sure drag this solid man to a dark corner and let him pull my wet panties aside.

I'm incredibly distracted, so much so that I jump when I see Beth right in front of me. Her eyes are wide, staring over my shoulder at the guy whose hand has shifted over my pelvic bone.

"What's your name?" Beth slurs loudly.

If his pinky slips just a little lower...

The man bends so Beth can hear him, making me shiver in delight when his scruff tickles my neck. "Felix!"

His answer is like a bucket of ice water being thrown over me. *I'm going to be sick.* Flinging myself away from him, I rush through the crowd with tears streaming down my cheeks.

I'm such an idiot. Many people have the same names as the assholes who broke my heart. The fact of the matter is, my sexual partners are nameless, so why would I stay?

That's what I tell myself as I scurry toward Kevin by the side entrance. I've had him on my radar all night, knowing where my safe place is. I really need my protector right now.

Four

FELIX

I can't get the image of that woman running away out of my head. I'm not sure what spooked her, but fuck was it disappointing to see her go.

Her blonde friend looked shocked to see her flee and immediately followed. I tried to give chase, but I could barely squeeze through the crowd. Those girls slipped through the sea of bodies like pros.

The way her body fit against mine and moved on me was a goddamn dream. Christ, she was sexy. I'm not ashamed to admit I had to rub one out as soon as I got home last night.

By the time I shoved my way off the dance floor, both the blue beauty and her friend were gone. Why the hell did she bolt, and where the hell did she go?

I only had her in my arms for a few minutes, but I can feel my obsession lingering. Going back and finding her will be easy. I have an interview there tonight, and she has bright blue hair. I'll spot her from a mile away.

Hopefully she's not someone visiting because I have

a feeling once with her won't be enough. I get what I want, and I want her.

Declan pokes my shoulder and stage whispers, "What are you daydreaming about?"

Glancing at him, I fight the urge to push his grinning face away from me. I like him close, but sometimes he makes me want to kick his ass. "This interview tonight."

"I call bullshit," Jared teases, eyeing the pillow on my lap. "You're thinking about wet pussy."

Ignoring the way Declan stiffens and moves away from me, I glare at my friend. "I didn't get any wet fuckin' pussy, so fuck off."

"So..." Jared drawls and swallows a bit of pasta salad. "You're pouting about the lack of wet pussy."

Fucking Christ. Jared and Declan are like the exact same person with their quick sass and outgoing personalities. There are a few key differences though, one being that Declan is a fucking troublemaker and Jared is a bit more calculated in his decision-making process.

I nudge Declan's thigh with my knee. "Declan, tell him to shut up." There, that should take the heat off of me. I don't love when they gang up on me, especially without Roman here to buffer their quips. But when Dec and Jared go at each other, everyone else ceases to exist. Only fiery sass and wicked jokes are their focus.

Except this time, my master plan to pin them against each other doesn't pan out how I expected. Declan stands and drags his hand through his dark brown hair. "Nah," He says, then leaves the room.

When a door slams further into the house, my gut

clenches. "What did I say wrong?" I ask Jared, feeling like a piece of shit.

Jared seems thoughtful when I catch him frowning. "I don't think that was necessarily about you."

"*Necessarily*?" Frustration fuels my tone, making Jared stiffen slightly.

The glare he levels at me is icy. "Yeah, Felix. You can't read someone for shit." Then he's up and storming out of the room too.

"What the fuck does that mean?" I grumble to myself and take a big gulp of my water.

At this point, I'd rather have a goddamn drink to chill my nerves, but showing up to an interview with a buzz wouldn't be a good idea.

Another door slams, making me cringe and reach for the joint tucked into my hat. *Goddamn it, I can't smoke either.* Living with three other guys hasn't always been easy, but moving from Seattle to Chicago has brought on a lot of stress.

Jared's dad got into an accident last year, and with Jared's natural inclination for anxiety, we decided to support him being close to his family. My parents are off traveling with Roman and Declan's parents, so nothing was really keeping us in Seattle anymore, anyway.

The sentimental ties didn't bother me because I was never close to my mom and dad. With my business degree and a decent amount of experience in management, I felt confident moving to another big city.

It was a bit harder for the Ledger brothers, Declan and Roman, to part ways with the place we grew up.

But if there's one thing the four of us have in common, it's loyalty. Jared needs his family nearby to feel settled, so yes, we all moved.

Four, thirty to thirty-three-year-old males moving across the country and into a packed city was quite the hassle, though. Loyalty runs really fucking deep, and it's been tested quite a bit this week.

Add in Declan managing a new family-owned cafe, Jared teaching at a new school, and me and Roman needing to find new jobs? We're pretty damn impatient with one another.

Also, I don't know who the hell said women were hormonal, because what I just witnessed in this damn living room screams *sensitive*. Or maybe I'm just a dick. Probably both.

I honestly don't know what I did wrong. Declan's always been weird about sex, especially when we're talking about our latest lays. Actually, I don't remember the last time he got some. I bet that's his problem.

Groaning at the thought of Dec getting some pussy, I hoist myself up and slam my water down on the coffee table. I need a nap, but I'd prefer a certain blue-haired bombshell.

I'll find her; I know it.

Five

BLUE

Working late nights has its perks, one of them being the option to hang out with Violet and my friends during the day.

Those plans have many drawbacks, though. Like the fact that I'm always so fucking tired. Whenever I plan a day to just sleep, it never actually happens.

Part of that has to do with the fact that I hate staying at home. After so many years forced into tiny shoebox homes with my aunt and cleaning up her messes, I get horribly antsy in my apartment.

Small spaces in general actually.

While mine and V's new apartment is *not* a shoebox, it's still an enclosed place filled with responsibilities. We have natural light, beautiful appliances, and cozy furniture, but there's still dishes to clean, floors to sweep, and the occasional lightbulb to change.

I have no idea how homeowners do it. Living with this crushing weight of having to take care of everything for an apartment is tiring. Especially when it's all on me to do it.

Since I was old enough to know what a mess was, I've had these responsibilities, and I'm a bit sick of the responsibility of being an adult.

I'm twenty-nine years old; I shouldn't feel this weighed down by life already. *Does anyone else feel this way?*

It helps to have active friends who like to go do stuff. Just last weekend we went to the art museum for fun. Then there's Violet, who never sits still and loves to explore. So yeah, I'm never home.

That brings me to now. Another hiking day with Violet has me yawning as I wiggle my way into a tight leather skirt.

The sun is down, Violet's getting ready for bed, and here I am trying to hype myself up to pour shots. Maybe I'll pound a quick vodka Red Bull before I go, and while I'm on break, a hard dicking sounds good. Rarely do I utilize the staff lounge when I'm working, but desperate times...

My vibrator died last night after replaying the dirty dancing I did with Felix. God, I hope it's a different Felix than the one I used to know.

Shifting my lacy top around to push my tits out more, I huff at my reflection. I don't love feeling bloated when I need to dress skimpy, but it is what it is. My blue hair is in some ratty curls tonight that fall haphazardly to the tops of my nipples, and I've forgone a necklace because my cleavage is pretty decent right now.

Leaving my room, I nudge Violet's hamper to the

side of the hallway and enter the kitchen. I grab the supplies I need to just fucking *get* me to work.

"Kay," I whisper, and jump up and down in three short bursts. A mixed drink isn't on my radar anymore. Instead I take a swig of Titos, then chase it with Red Bull.

"Have a good night!" is shouted from the other side of the apartment.

I cough a little and wipe my mouth. "You too!"

As much as I long to crawl into bed, I can't. There's a plan in place to change my schedule. I just have to hold on a little longer.

I can sleep when I'm dead.

Closing shifts are always easier when Mark, our bar manager, is MIA. What makes working really great is having me, Beth, and Janine behind the bar until close too.

Tonight is one of those nights. Plus, Saturdays always breeze by because the music is being run by our favorite DJ, and the crowd is drunker which means...ding, ding, ding! You guessed it! More tips.

Everyone knows you don't get too fucked up on Fridays to save yourself for Saturdays.

Snatching a twenty-dollar bill from the wet bar top before the drunk idiot realizes how much he tipped me,

I grin and twist away. Janine fist bumps me, and we're right back to it.

Sometimes I feel bad for mooching off their drunkenness, but when someone only speaks to my boobs, yeah, I'll take their ridiculously large tip. *Thank you. See you next time!*

The girls and I give great service, so we deserve the appreciation, even if it wasn't soberly intentional. Our awesome reputation is proven when a regular Saturday college student drapes herself over the bar.

With a big smile, Dani shouts, "Hi, Blue!"

"Hi, baby!" I bounce over to her and offer her a free bottle of water. When I first met her last year, I jokingly called her *baby* because she had a baby face. She's really grown into herself this year, and I'll be sad if she moves away after graduation.

"How're you?" she slurs and chugs the water.

I grab her another water, loving how she lets me look after her without question. "Same ole. Did you pass your psych exam?"

Her big green eyes widen, and she squeals. "YES! Thank you for all the advice!"

My mood lifts. "Fuck yeah! Good job, baby!" I didn't do much in the way of helping, just gave her some good websites to guide her studying.

"DANI!" another girl screeches, grabbing Dani by the hips and dragging her back onto the dance floor. Sweet girl that she is, Dani lets her friend drag her away with a wave goodbye.

I laugh and wiggle my fingers at her. Sometimes when

I think about Dani, jealousy flares up. Freshly twenty-one, following her dreams of becoming a therapist and enjoying the college life, Dani's living the life I wish had been an option for me when I finished high school.

Heat engulfs my hand and pulls it back down to the counter. "What's a man got to do to get your attention, huh?"

That voice.

I'm too stunned to yank my hand away from his grasp, and when Beth slides in next to me, I suck in a breath. "It's your break. And good timing, huh?" she whispers, and rushes to help another man.

How is he *here?*

I let my burning eyes follow the path of his muscular arm, up to his shoulder, and get stuck on his chiseled face. Dirty blond hair in disarray, sinful smirk, and tattoos poking beneath his V-neck. Felix, the boy who left me in an abusive home, stares back like he has no idea who I am.

"It was so easy to find you." My tummy sinks with his words. *He was looking for me?* "I'd recognize your blue hair anywhere after having it draped over my chest last night."

Fuck, so it *was* him. Rage burns hot and thick in my skull, but what he says next has me disassembling my explosion.

"What's your name, doll?"

The rage that tried to consume me now wraps around me in a coat of armor. Felix is not a boy anymore. No, this is a fucking man in front of me. One who doesn't recognize the girl he broke and left to fend for herself.

The boy who was once my friend is now a man I'll torment.

I grin and all but shove my tits in his face. "My name is Blue. *Pleasure*."

Felix's eyes heat, which is something I never got to witness in my teen years. He's a goddamn tank, and once I drag him down, I'll feel so much fucking better.

"Pleasure's all—"

I cut the bastard off with a finger to his plump lips. "Mine. The pleasure is mine, Felix."

The bouncy energy I had minutes ago boosts me up onto the bar. Swinging my legs around while keeping hold of Felix, I prepare for him to fight me. But he doesn't.

Felix is still the same stupid boy he used to be. He can dress up in black jeans, a backwards hat, and a tight black shirt, but he's still a fucking asshole with a one-track mind.

Smirking to myself, I weave us through the throngs of people until we reach the staff lounge. Once I've gotten what I need, I'm going to shatter his selfish heart.

Should have been more careful, doll.

Six

FELIX

Holy fucking shit, this chick is sexy.

She hesitated for only a second when I grabbed her hand, but she hasn't let go yet. In all honesty, I'm feeling slightly intimidated by her confidence right now.

Don't get me wrong, my cock is hard, and I'm willingly following her toward the back of the club. All thoughts of my interview flew out the window when I caught sight of my blue beauty.

My?

I don't have long to think about my ludicrous claiming before she yanks me into a cozy lounge that I didn't know existed. Just like I barely had a chance to figure out why she seemed familiar before she stole my breath with her *pleasure* innuendo.

"Fuck, you're hot," I groan as I'm shoved back into the door. The valley between her breasts is so damn enticing in the low, warm lighting. Over her shoulder, I see a few red couches and a small seating area by a wall of mirrors. *This room was meant for sex.*

"Thanks," she says, kissing my collarbone. I'm not sure if it's the fact that I feel like I'm out of my depth right now, but she sounds sarcastic.

Blue strands of hair tickle my jaw, making me feel like a damn king with our height difference. Pressure around my hips forces me to buck into her tight stomach. I hiss, holding back my impending orgasm while she grips my belt and maneuvers me.

I'm under her spell. "Your name's Blue?" *The fuck is wrong with me?* Why do I care? I have a sexy fucking woman in front of me ready for my cock. *There's something about her...*

"Yep. Stop talking," she basically snarls and bites my peck through my shirt.

I jolt, and my cock drips. "Shit!"

Blue grins but still doesn't look up at me. I feel like I'm just a hot body to her. Which should be great, but I want to push her back and ask her about her damn day. *What the actual fuck?!*

"What's your last name, Blue?"

My head slams back against the door when heat engulfs my cock. Just feeling her hand through my jeans makes me fucking dizzy.

A noise huffs from the beautiful Blue, snapping me out of my lust-induced haze. *God, I can't come yet.*

"It's my turn if we're playing twenty questions."

Her response to my question startles me, but there's a flicker of excitement at playing this game with her. "Go ahead, doll."

Kneeling before me, Blue pulls my pants down until they're around my knees. Still, she won't fucking look at me. Instead she murmurs her question to my weeping cock tenting my boxers. "What is your greatest quality, Felix? Something everyone would agree with."

I don't have to think about it. *But I should have.* "I'm fiercely loyal."

Then, as if the entire world holds its breath, the blue goddess on her knees before me *finally* looks me in the eye. Unlike the rest of the world, I don't think I'll take another breath again.

Slowly, as if threatening me, she stands. Those ice-blue eyes that I dream about every motherfucking night stare me down with a fiery rage that I never would have expected from my childhood friend.

"Erica..." I breathe, shocked and completely devastated. Nothing else infiltrates my mind, no questions of how she's here right now, or wondering why she's with me. All I can think about is how much I've missed her. "Eri—"

"I disagree," Erica cuts me off. While her eyes are filled with absolute rage and hurt, her beautiful face is cold and shut off. "I completely disagree, Felix. You aren't loyal."

I open my mouth, but she steps back and waves her hand as if to silence me. "You lied to me now, just like you did then. *I'll always be here for you, Erica, no matter how far away I am.*"

I remember promising her that. She was sixteen and sad that I didn't go to the same school as her. Erica was struggling with her home life, and I always did everything I could to help her.

Until I didn't.

"Erica," I plead, reaching for her, only to crash to my knees because where else would I be? I'm exactly where I deserve to be. On my knees with my pants holding me in place in front of my first love. My *only* love.

Her lips curl, breaking the cool facade. "My name is *Blue*, asshole."

But she's not. Her name is Erica.

"You know," she giggles, and my heart thumps in tune with her anger. "You were the last one I spoke to. The last one who blocked me."

"I—"

"You don't get to speak!" she screams, then turns away from me but not before I see the tears streaming down her cheeks. "Where was *loyal* Felix when I begged him to help me? When I told him my aunt's new boyfriend was hurting me, huh? Where was this loyalty when I feared I might be *sexually assaulted?!*"

No...She couldn't have been...

"Where was your loyalty?! *WHERE WERE YOU,* FELIX?!"

A gunshot to my heart would have hurt less. "Erica—"

Whirling around, Erica looks fucking feral and *destroyed*. "NO! My name is *Blue!* Erica died a long ass time ago."

I didn't think I could feel any worse, but when she wipes her cheeks and straightens her shoulders, I die inside. Begging her to stop would be wrong, but, fucking hell, I feel like she's filleting me from the inside out.

"You, Jared, Declan, and Roman let sweet Erica go, and so did I. Except the difference between you and me? I didn't have a choice. You *chose* to abandon me to a line of abusive predators."

"No—"

She rushes me, fury and so much pain twisting her beauty. "Just shut up! Stop! What makes you think you have any right to invalidate my feelings or the horrors I survived?!"

Kill me now.

"Goodbye, Felix."

Wait WHAT?!

A soft breeze tickles my cheek, sending my panic higher as my girl leaves. When the door slams in my face, I finally snap out of it, only to trip over my fucking jeans and crash into the wall.

"Fuck!"

What have I done?

Seven

BLUE

No, no, no! This can't be happening!

That wasn't the plan. Not at all. I was *maybe* going to get a few orgasms before leaving him high and dry like he did to me. Now it's all ruined. I can't believe I caved so fast, but as soon as he spouted that shit about loyalty being his best quality, I snapped.

The only time I ever raise my voice is when I'm being threatened or when someone else is, which does happen frequently at the club here. I'm usually swinging a steel fucking water bottle at them too.

How could I have been so stupid as to leave with Felix while being defenseless? I should have known he would break me before I was ready. And, oh my God, do I feel fucking shattered right now.

Bethany and Janine are about to lose their shit.

"What happened?!" Bethany screeches, running up to me and immediately wiping the tears from my cheeks.

I shake my head, my lip wobbling. Words don't come out, but having my water bottle clutched in my grip helps calm me.

Then Janine sees me. Anger and fear morph her features into something I've never seen from her. "Tell me," she demands.

I have to appreciate the new layers we're allowing each other to see. These girls have never seen me about to have a meltdown, nor have they needed to come running to my rescue. It's always the other way around.

Shaking my head again, I hiccup and glance over my shoulder. "Not now. I have to go."

Bethany hesitates, but Janine nods and grabs my purse. "Go. But please keep us in the loop."

Grateful, I hug them both tight and fast, then I'm fucking gone. I can't wait around for Felix to pull his pants up and come after me. *He didn't then, so why would he now?*

My tears flow freely as I rush through the crowd. *Why the hell is he here?! Oh fuck, are all four of them in town?*

Just as a frustrated scream builds in the back of my throat, a familiar broad back enters my line of sight. A rush of air escapes me as I whisper my friend's name and scurry behind his big frame.

The voice that acts as a balm to my wounds isn't Kevin's like I anticipated. "Blue? Oh shit, are you crying?!" Levi, Kevin's husband and my personal trainer, gasps as he reaches for me.

Kevin stiffens beside Levi, registering the anguish

probably written all over my face. Both of them make the perfect buff protective wall. *Is he looking for me?*

I choke, relieved to have both him and Kev surrounding me. Gathering the courage to tell them what's wrong isn't as hard as I thought it would be, but it helps that they already know most of what's happened to me growing up.

"One of them...Felix. He-He's here," I stutter and curl in on myself. The chill of my Stanley water bottle shocks me out of the incoming panic attack.

Before I realize what's happening, Levi and Kevin each have one arm wrapped around me. I follow along mindlessly as they direct me to the security room and onto the leather couch.

Sweat makes the back of my neck itch, and the leather skirt is a fucking nuisance at this point. Sexy, fun, and carefree no longer fit my mental state.

"I'll drive her home," Levi's voice breaks through the sound of music thumping through the walls. "She shouldn't drive like this." Kevin agrees with a grunt.

My answer is instinctual, even though they weren't asking. "I'm fine."

"Shut up," Kevin scolds as he crouches in front of me. "You look like shit. You're going home, resting this off, and coming up with a plan if this jackass is sticking around."

If it were anyone else saying this shit to me, I'd be offended and pissed off. But Kevin has always been abrasive and rude—that's just his charm.

"And," Levi chimes in with a pointed look. "Scheduling a time to have a legit chat about this."

I stiffen. "There's nothing much to say. I brought him to the employee lounge to get some O's, then he pissed me off. Unfortunately for him, he realized who I was far too late to redeem himself."

"In my fucking opinion," Kevin growls, "the four of them don't deserve redemption."

Smirking, even though it's sad, I tease the couple. "You sure you don't swing my way? Because I'd love this kind of devotion in a relationship."

Levi snorts. "Been there, almost done you, Blue."

At that, I really do laugh. Seven years ago, Levi and I messed around for like two weeks. We never had sex because he was shying away from it. Enter Kevin, the new broody guy at the gym, then finally everything made sense. Levi preferred men, and it just so happened Kevin was exactly his type.

Was I shocked when Levi broke things off with me because he was more interested in a man? Not really. I could literally feel their connection.

Kev chuckles good-naturedly. "I'm still glad your last fling was Blue. Best thing that came out of your uncertainty was our friendship and you waiting for me."

Levi blushes, and I swear to shit I swoon for them. It's a cliché to say *they are goals*, but there's nothing else to say. Both are big, strong, steely men, but for each other they melt like chocolate on a nipple for Valentine's Day.

Yes, that can happen.

My heart constricts when they kiss. Not because I want either of them in that way but because I want what they have. It's hard to find that when I'm closed off to relationships and anything more than a one-night stand, though.

"Blue's getting blue..." Levi whispers.

That observation of my mood and weeping eyes makes me curl into a ball on the couch. What he just said...*Blue's getting blue*...is the exact reason I legally changed my name to this when I was eighteen.

What I told Felix about happy Erica being gone was the truth. Instead of yellow sunflowers, I became wilted blue petals with no stem to survive off of. Blue as in melancholy. Blue as in sadness.

Because no matter how much I party or adventure with the people who love me, I'm still really fucking sad.

"Come on, Blue," Levi coos, pulling me from the security room couch. "Let's get you home."

On the ride home with Levi, all I can think about is that I don't think I'll ever stop being sad for the girl who came before this hardened version of myself.

Even wilted and dead, I still feel pain. Felix proved that tonight when he so casually forgot about his betrayal.

Where was his loyalty when I needed it the most?

Eight

DECLAN

Felix came home late last night. It's noon, and he's still sleeping. I'm starting to get annoyed not only with myself for my feelings but with him. *What the hell was he doing last night?* Or *who*?

My jealousy spirals the longer he doesn't show.

"You good?" Jared nudges me, looking concerned.

I shrug. This past year has been hell trying to understand how I feel about Felix. He's always been my older brother's best friend and became a really good friend of mine too.

Yet, he's become more than that in the past few years. I find myself watching him, hoping he catches me looking so he can give me more attention. Craving Felix is uncomfortably inconvenient.

Why? Because he fucks anything that looks nice, and my balls have been blue for about eight months. The sultry looks I get from women are nice, but when Felix's eyes are on me, I'm on fucking fire.

Jared sighs, tipping his head back against the couch.

His brown skin stretches over his Adam's apple when he swallows, but it doesn't do anything for me. The only man I have the hots for is someone who views me as a kid brother.

Fuck my life.

"You're destined to be celibate for the rest of your life."

"Fuck," I grumble, rubbing my hand over my scruff. "I know. The last time I tried the woman was too soft and sweet."

Jared snorts. "I didn't realize there was such a thing."

"Such a thing as what?" Roman asks, wandering into the living room with a protein shake.

I scowl at Jared for his loud mouth, but he pays me no mind, still reclined back on the couch. "Nothing," I answer my brother.

Roman levels me with a flat look but brushes it off and leaves the room again. I wonder if he's going to scout out another gym. Guilt builds in my chest. *Did I upset him?*

Three years older than me, Roman is the role model he worked hard to become. Strong, smart, calm, and kind. He's the whole package for anyone willing to endure his tortured soul.

What do I have to offer Felix? Sass, snark, and impulsivity.

"You have to tell him." Jared sounds bored and slightly annoyed. I don't blame him. We've had this argument many times.

"No," I mumble, "I really don't."

Jared sits up and looks me in the eye. "Listen, D, he's

going to find out sooner or later." My heart sinks, but my friend continues. "He will. Then he's going to feel like shit that he didn't notice."

"Well, that's fucking embarrassing as it is. I think we'll just keep this to ourselves. Want to get dinner?" Divert. Avoid. Ignore. It will pass.

Jared rolls his eyes and stands. "Asshole, you know I can't pass up a good burger. Let's go see my sister first, please. She's at work."

I'm already nodding as I grab the keys. Another great part of moving here is finally seeing Jared's sister again. She's ten years older and moved to Chicago when she was twenty-six, so we haven't seen her much in the past thirteen years.

Excitement urges me out of the house while muting my anxiety about Felix. For now. My dilemma and nauseating jealousy will come roaring back later, but for now, I'm thrilled to be seeing Nichole again.

"You drive," I demand and toss Jared the keys to my Toyota Camry. "I'm feeling distracted."

Jared agrees, and we're off to visit his sister.

The drive isn't far, but the traffic through downtown Chicago is ridiculous. "Jesus Christ, why does your sister like working in this mess?" I ask as we dodge people along the sidewalk.

We drove less than three miles, and still have to

walk a third of one because of the shit parking. Thank fuck my café has its own parking lot.

"She said the location brings great business. People can come before work, during lunch breaks, or after work. Add in the nice locker rooms she updated last year, and her customers can freshen up. It's one of the hottest studios in the city."

"Makes sense." It does, especially once I see the gorgeous glass storefront with a striking purple and blue logo. "Damn, I hadn't seen the updates. Did you get pictures?"

Jared nods, and I glare as I follow him inside. "Sorry, it was around the time Dad got into the accident."

"Shit," I cringe, feeling like an insensitive ass. "I'm sorry. I didn't think about the timing. It looks fucking awesome in here."

It feels glorious too. The air is crisp, and the entry room is super inviting. There's complimentary fruit and water near the waiting area, and the receptionist is beaming.

"Hi, welcome in! How can I help you?" She's cute, in a bubbly kind of way. All I feel though is the usual guilt and heartache when I encounter someone so outwardly happy. *Erica was like that.*

"Hey," Jared greets. "I'm visiting my sister, Nichole. Is she around?"

"Oh!" She smiles. "You're Jared. Nikki told me to keep an eye out for you this week! She's just finishing up her evening class, but she'll be out in a few minutes, I bet. Nikki always walks out with them to keep chatting."

The obvious respect this girl has for Nichole makes me smile. *Nikki* has done well for herself it seems, and I couldn't be happier for her.

"Great, thank you," Jared acknowledges and takes a seat on the couch.

I follow suit, grabbing an orange on my way toward him. "When's the last time we saw Nichole do you think? I can't remember."

"It's been a long while. Maybe like eight months, but we didn't see her much. We were busy house hunting, remember?"

"Oh shit, yeah." I cross my right leg over my knee and dig my nail into the skin of my orange. Just as I'm about to ask how she's been doing, the double doors burst open in a flurry of laughter, thumping music, and sweaty women.

"JARED!" Nichole screams and runs right for her brother. He jumps up and swoops her into a tight embrace. "I'm so happy you're here," she cries.

I smile and approach them slowly. With a piece of peel in my hand, I reach to drop it in the garbage. Instead of releasing the skin, I drop the whole damn orange when my eyes catch on my living fucking nightmare.

She may have blue hair and angry eyes now, but I would recognize her anywhere anytime.

"Erica..."

Nine

BLUE

I knew if Felix was in town, the others most likely were as well. Hoping they were just visiting for the weekend didn't do much to curb the anxiety I've felt about seeing more of them.

My nerves after my run-in with Felix last night have been buzzing with anticipation. Almost as if my instincts knew before I was ready to admit that everything was about to change.

So, with my day off and nothing to do, I cycled this morning and this evening. Levi wasn't available at the gym, and I needed the vibes of hyped-up women to perk me up a little. He promised to pick me up and take me to get a snack after.

Walking out the doors with a group of empowered women with music following us was exactly what I needed. Knowing Levi is probably walking up as we speak helps me stay positive. Right up until Nichole's identity slaps me across the face.

Wrapped in Jared's muscled arms, Nichole cries in

relief. Meanwhile, my soul is fucking bleeding, and tears spring to my eyes.

How could this be? Obviously I knew my high school friend had an older sister who moved away, but what are the damn odds?!

My tears dry right the fuck up as burning hot rage heats my heart. The sadness and longing I felt a moment ago scatters to the wind like ash. In no fucking universe do these self-absorbed pricks deserve anything but anger from me.

Yet, the scared seventeen-year-old still inside of me cries and wraps her arms around herself. *How could they leave me?* All these years later and I'm still asking the same questions.

A dull thud accompanied by a choked gasp of a name that no longer exists draws my attention. *Declan.* Still the pretty boy of the group. Dark scruff shaped to perfection around his sharp jawline. Of course he'd have a basic man haircut with his dark brown hair long on top and short on the sides. His thin pink lips are open in shock.

What he does next absolutely fucking baffles me. Declan, my ex partner in crime and first one to betray me, smiles. *Fucking smiles!*

I'm going to kill him. That thought comes really close to reality when Declan rushes me with his arms wide open.

"Erica, holy shit!" He beams, acting as if he didn't randomly start icing me out in senior year. As if he didn't give me enough scraps of friendship to keep me hooked, only to drop me completely when I moved.

Leave me alone, Erica. Move on.

With the memory of horrible rejection, I retaliate against his unwanted reunion. Since my emotions are roiling at the surface, all my self-defense training flies right out the damn window. My failure to remember everything Levi and Kevin have taught me is something I never could have predicted.

I should knee Declan in the balls, or twist to the side and trip him at the last second, but I don't do any of those things.

His scent of manly aftershave assaults my senses, and his large hands coming closer send me into an angry panic. With my hands wide and my elbows bent, I push him with all my might. I don't account for the fact that Declan is no longer a skinny teenager. He's a solid man.

My miscalculation of Declan's strength and momentum cost me. With my hands splayed on his chest, I stumble back as my left wrist tweaks with a sharp zing of pain.

"Shit!" I cry and yank my hands back to cradle my injured one against my sweaty chest.

"Are you okay?!" Declan sounds panicked and far too close.

Looking up at him while I'm hurt and vulnerable reminds me of the last time he knew I was in a similar position. Hurt and vulnerable. His response was to leave me all alone. *How could he?*

"Don't touch me," I spit, ignoring the way my throat closes over with so much emotion I feel like I'm going to drown.

Declan frowns and reaches for me. "Erica—"

"She asked you not to fucking touch her, you son of a bitch."

My exhale of pure relief is grounding. Shifting, I rush to Levi's side passing a frozen Jared. *I'm so fucking weak.*

Declan's demeanor changes the moment he sees me standing next to my sexy *married* best friend. "Who the fuck are you?" he demands.

Levi clenches his fists. "Who the fuck are *you*? You always put your hands on women who tell you no?"

"WHAT?!" Jared booms, finally snapping out of his shock I guess, and runs over to stand beside Declan.

Nichole inches between us and them slightly. "Levi, this is Jared, my brother. And Declan, my brother's best friend," she says softly, trying to diffuse the situation.

It's then I realize we're alone; the rest of the class probably has been ushered outside.

Levi doesn't take his eyes off Declan. "I don't care. Blue said no."

"Blue?" Pissed off and perplexed, Declan demands answers. "Erica, what the fuck is going on?"

There's something utterly soul crushing about hearing my name come from Declan's mouth. With Felix, it was easy to snap at him, but with Declan, all I feel is so much hurt I can barely breathe.

"Erica, baby..." Jared murmurs as his hand lifts toward me. "Your hair..."

Just like that, the deep sadness I felt because of Declan, turns into hysteria. A laugh bursts from my throat without warning. *How dare he comment on my hair like it fucking offended him?*

Old ladies with zero creativity can scoff all they want at my choice of style, but this asshole? He's lost all right to even fucking *look* at me.

"Get out." My voice is strong and steady. I'm coaxing the broken parts of me back into their safe places. *I'll let them out once I'm alone.*

Both Jared and Declan frown at my demand. "What?" they question in unison.

"I said, *get out.*"

They don't move except for the twitch of their jaws. These damn idiots still seem lost. I'll spell it out for them then.

Straightening my spine and lifting my chin, I allow my resilience to take over. In a fuzzy haze of trying to keep my heartbreak at bay and zoning out their masculine features, I make it so they won't have any question of where we stand.

"I don't want to see you, hear you, speak to you, let alone *touch* you ever again. Feel free to pass the message to the other two as well. If you're here to stay, I'll find a different studio, because unlike some people, I wouldn't be so heartless as to keep you away from family."

Nichole gasps, and my heart thumps an extra sad beat. "Blue, you don't have to—"

"I do," I cut her off. "He's your brother, but I will *not* associate myself and V with their brand of cruelty."

"Now wait a fucking second!" Declan snaps, pointing a finger at me like I'm a damn child.

Levi's quick to shut that shit down. "Don't fucking point at her."

To Nichole, I tell her in words she might understand. "I won't subject myself or Violet to the men who left me alone with my aunt."

Tears fill Nichole's eyes, and her hand flies to her mouth. Rounding on Jared, she stares at him as if he's a stranger. "That was *you*?"

I'm stingy with information and tend to avoid offering details. Names were never provided. She would never have known because there's a dark part of me I refuse to share with everyone.

Nichole and I didn't realize our connection until I saw her run into her brother's arms. Watching her put the pieces of my trauma together and realizing the turning point in my life could have been much better if her brother and his friends had been there for me is upsetting.

I don't want to hurt my friend, and that's not my intention. I need her to let me go. Nichole is a spitfire and will do everything she can to keep me coming back here. I hope now she might cut me some slack.

Pressure on my bicep brings me one step closer to breaking. Levi leans down and catches my eye. "You okay? You zoned out."

I nod, but my eyes tell him no. He understands me immediately—*I need to leave.*

"Nichole, we're leaving. Don't let those two follow us out." With that, Levi wraps an arm around my waist and guides me to the door.

Jared and Declan protest, but they sound muffled behind the anguish building in my body.

I'm about to break, please just don't let it be in front of them.

"Violet's calling me," Levi says as we approach the glass door. I don't realize what he's doing until he answers it on speakerphone.

My girl's twinkly voice comes through the speakers, loudly. "Are you with Mama?"

"Yeah, kiddo. She's right here," Levi answers, then hands the phone to me so he can open the studio door and keep an arm around me.

I follow him outside, unaware of the chaos we're leaving in our wake.

Ten

JARED

My chest feels like it's gone ten rounds with a fucking gorilla. My feet are screaming at me to run after the girl I've missed every single day since she moved.

Yet, I'm frozen by my sister's dark tear-filled eyes. Betrayal and hurt dull the brilliance that is Nichole.

"I—"

"Do you know what they did to her?" my sister cuts me off. The pain in my chest heightens with all the possibilities of what Erica may have suffered in our absence. *What the hell happened?!*

"Nichole—"

She steps back. "Why did you do that? *How* could you do that, Jared? You've always been a sweet, thoughtful person. Even as a boy!"

I'm torn between spilling the truth to my sister and chasing Erica out the door. Before I can decide which course of action to take, a new voice catches my attention.

"Are you with Mama?"

Mama? Scrutinizing the scene by the door, I listen to that buff prick, Levi, speak into his phone. "Yeah, kiddo. She's right here."

No. My heart falls right out of my ass when Levi hands Erica the phone. *Mama?*

"What the fuck?" Declan whispers, sounding strangled.

"Hey, sweetheart." Erica's voice is soft and suddenly so patient I yearn for that kind of attention from her. "I'm coming home instead. Okay, love you."

Then they're fucking gone.

The silence left in their wake is so tense chills break out across my skin. The past five minutes feel like a goddamn blur.

I was so excited to see my sister and make summer plans now that we're in the same city again. Being taller than Nichole didn't make me feel older when she held onto me. The little boy, whose sister moved away too soon, came skipping to the surface ready for more adventures.

Then Declan said a name I hadn't heard pass his lips in *so* long. I thought I had imagined it, but one quick look to the side and there she was. Erica Bennett. The girl we loved and ghosted.

I felt as if I were stuck in slow motion. Dec rushed toward her...Erica attempted to stop him. I watched, helpless and horrified, when panic twisted her features, then her wrist.

Once again, she was hurt because of us.

I should have stopped Declan from pursuing her

when she was cowering away. Then she fucking fled toward another man for safety. Everything I witnessed was so *wrong.*

Erica always ran to *us* when she needed something. I know I shouldn't blame her for pushing Declan away, and I don't. I blame myself, which is so much fucking worse.

Then she asked us to go, only to take it back and say *she* would go and not come back to my sister's cycling class. In that moment, I felt guilty for making my sister lose a customer. *Then* I realized they were goddamn friends!

As if things couldn't get worse, all Erica had to do was say *one* sentence for my sister to stiffen in accusation and shock.

Erica called us cruel. I so badly want to deny it and defend myself, but my subconscious wholeheartedly agrees. I've had nightmares and so many moments of worry over what could have been happening to Erica.

Of course, one final bit of information that I never could have guessed landed like a steel knife in my windpipe. I feel so nauseated, horrified, and truly upset that Erica has a child, my knees wobble.

"SHE HAS A KID?!" Declan bellows on the verge of yanking his hair out. His question is aimed at both of us, but my sister is the only one who has the answer.

Nichole's eyebrows twitch before they furrow in an icy look that freezes my veins. Death feels like it's coming for me through my big sister's glare.

"Tell me. Please?" I beg Nichole, ready to get on my knees for any scrap of information about Erica.

"I don't want to tell you *shit*, Jared. This is so fucked up."

"What's fucked up is our woman has a kid with another man!" Declan shouts.

Declan will most definitely not be okay in public once we leave here. He's hyperventilating, probably recalling all the times during senior year we dismissed Erica and ignored her. Distancing ourselves from the girl we loved was awful, but we thought it would make the split easier.

It didn't.

"You're going to tell me everything you guys did before I give you even a *sliver* of Blue." Nichole is furious and protective, making me realize there's no getting past her boundaries.

"Who the hell is Blue and what the fuck was up with Erica and that dickhead?" Declan spits.

I'm one second away from forcing him to rein in his attitude because even though Nichole is not on our side for once, that doesn't give him the right to disrespect her.

Nichole crosses her arms. She looks like a warrior ready to throw down on behalf of her friend. I'm so glad Erica found her way to Nichole, even if it was by coincidence.

"You call her Erica. Everyone in Chicago calls her Blue. As it is on her ID. Erica, whoever that was, doesn't exist here. I suggest you realize what that means before approaching Blue again."

"Sh-She changed her name?"

Nichole's chin lifts in defiance. "Like I said. I need to

know you aren't completely horrible when it comes to Blue before I say shit."

Declan curses and begins to pace.

She's looking at us as if we really are cruel.

Is it cruel to want to rip Erica's baby daddy apart and take his place in her life?

Probably.

But the disappointment from my role model won't stop me from making amends and bringing our girl back into our arms.

Fuck it, *I am cruel.*

She demanded we let her go, and there's no scenario I would ever make that mistake again. I'm not letting Erica go.

We need to tell the others.

Eleven

BLUE

I cried and cried and cried last night. Violet's snuggles and Levi's encouraging words got me through the night, but still...I haven't broken down like that in years.

My eyes burn today, and unfortunately, they're the only thing I need to work right now. Studying the policies and rules for the security team is proving to be a difficult feat.

I love working as a bartender, but when I heard that our head of security is retiring, something inside me lit up. An idea sparked to life three months ago, and the support I've received from everyone lit the fuse.

I'm a natural leader with enough defensive skills that I might just be able to run security for Serpent's Kiss. Because I've worked here for a long ass time, I know the building and our customers like the back of my hand.

Though I might not have the training to be a bouncer or security guard, I sure as hell know the team.

I've been studying them, their blind spots, their strengths and placement preferences. Not being one of them might be a problem, but that's why I have to pass this test with flying colors.

I'm ready for something new. For eleven years, I've been a bartender—I don't want my background to be booze anymore.

Doubling down on my notes, I barely notice Kevin dropping off another coffee. He's been instrumental in helping me fill in the gaps that I can't get from reading manuals.

I focus and soak as much in as I can for...*Shoot, what time is it?*

"Blue! We're opening!" Janine shouts, poking her head into the office.

"Shit!" I jump up, shove my stuff into my backpack and dash to the bathroom to change. Cotton shorts and a sweatshirt aren't appropriate clothes for work.

Breaking a sweat as I shimmy into a pair of leather pants and a sparkly silver bra is incredibly common. I regret the pants, but I didn't pack anything else. "It's fine," I huff and fluff my bright blue hair up.

My combat booties will be fun tonight, at least. With my trusty water bottle, I lock my backpack away in our lounge and rush for the bar.

Sexy, messy, and ready to get people drunk. *Let's go.*

At least I don't close tonight. I repeat that over and over in my head. Sometimes I wish we were a normal club that's only open on weekends until I remember that wouldn't pay the bills.

One big thing that sets Serpent's Kiss apart from the other nightlife of Chicago is that we're open seven days a week. We're in the center of downtown, with constant college kids and people visiting for more than just Cloud Gate, also known as The Bean, or our pizza.

Someone has to give these people a good time, and that's us. It's exhausting, but at least I have Tuesdays and Wednesdays off. Those are our slowest days since they seem to be the days people travel home. Monday through Thursday we close at one in the morning; the other nights are three A.M.

Our owners are looking into getting a Late Hour Liquor License which would allow us to close at five in the morning. *Gross.*

For a Monday, it's ridiculously busy here. My feet are dying. I should have stuck to my tennis shoes. At least I'm off early. Do I wish I could always clock out before midnight? Yes. I'm just trying to be grateful that I can tonight.

Then I have two days off. Just an hour and a half left.

"How are those leather pants treating you?" Janine teases while wiping sweat from her brow with a paper towel.

I flip her off. "Mondays aren't supposed to be *this* wild."

Maybe there's some sort of festival or concert nearby

that I missed. My brain has been yanking me off track since dancing with Felix last Friday.

"I'm starving," I complain to Bethany a short while later.

It's not Bethany who replies, though. Four men, the ones who star in all my nightmares, sidle up to the bar with varying looks of caution and determination. Declan eyes my gauze wrapped wrist with so much guilt I have to look away.

"Come take a break with us, Erica."

Of course it's Felix who *demands* something from me. All thoughts of devouring a dozen tacos or a whole pizza shrivel up in gut-roiling annoyance.

Beth stiffens in solidarity with me. I told my girl-friends a bit of what was going on before cycling last night. No details or much backstory. Just that some guys from high school were bothering me. For the first time since waking up this morning, I'm grateful I cried out all of my goddamn tears. Now all I have to offer is exhaustion and anger.

"I told you to leave me alone. And my name is Blue," I state, cracking open a White Claw and handing it to a customer.

Never did I think Felix, Declan, Jared, and Roman would be standing at my bar. I feel sick and like I'm about to crawl out of my skin. They're violating my happy place.

"Erica..."

Roman...

To say I'm shocked at the pain I hear in his voice is an understatement. What does he have to be upset about right now? Maybe he doesn't like my hair like Jared or some shit.

A strobe light flashes across Roman, and what I see has me sucking in a gasp. Colorless flowers are tattooed around the sides of his neck. *For me? No! He wouldn't do that.*

Snapping my eyes up, I take in the rest of him. Dark shaggy hair and pale skin, Roman is wider and slightly taller than the other three. He's built to hurt, but the soft, scared look on his scruffy face says the opposite.

"You're great at ignoring me, aren't you, Roman?" It's a jab, and it makes him flinch just as I had hoped. Obviously he's ignoring my wishes and my new name, but that was meant to be deeper. He ignored all my texts—completely ghosted me like Jared.

As the most mature one in our group growing up, I expected more from him. Clearly, he doesn't have the balls to be a fucking man. Not back then, and not now either, it seems.

"Petal..." Roman croaks, leaning over the bar.

Throwing my wrapped wrist up in the air, I halt him from doing any more damage. *Petal...his nickname for me.*

Bethany wraps an arm around my hip, giving me the strength to reply. "We don't serve assholes. Get out."

"Blue, babe!"

Son of a motherfucking bitch. Pasting on a fake as shit smile, I wave at our regular. Bethany swoops in to deal with it, thank hell. "I'll get your usual, Dale!" she titters and goes about making him a Captain and Coke.

"Thanks." Dale doesn't even spare Beth a glance as he drapes himself across the bar next to Felix. Already drunk, Dale doesn't fail to make an ass out of himself. "Blue, how 'bout that shot tonight, hmm?"

His slurring makes me cringe. "Not tonight. We're too busy."

A dark look fills his eyes. "Seriously? Just one shot. You fucking owe me, bitch."

Then all hell breaks loose.

Twelve

ROMAN

Pinned by familiar bright blue eyes, I remember all the ways I've failed Erica. I always knew the decisions I made as a selfish eighteen-year-old would come back to haunt me. It didn't take long either.

About a week and a half after deleting Erica's phone number, I began to suffocate in the aftermath of my decision. I'll forever hate myself for letting her go without a word, but damn my parents were convincing when they told me the damage had already been done and I shouldn't drag her around anymore.

I believed them. Then they sent me off to college with a credit card in their name and a ton of encouragement to figure out who I wanted to be. I took their distraction and pushed myself to be an accomplished adult.

I went to the gym, took business courses for a while —enough to understand a few things—and started working. Felix moved in with me a few weeks after classes started and pushed me into new experiences, which became another distraction. My best friend was spiraling, and I jumped right into the chaos with him.

No matter how high I got, how much I drank, I still hated myself. So I worked fucking hard during the day to ease the guilt by telling myself I would help people someday. At night, I aimed to fill the void in my heart with chicks and music.

My parents never knew about my stupidity. Until Declan came to live with us a year later. A few too many drinks and a leap off a frat house sent him to the ER not six months into living with me and Felix. Idiot didn't land correctly in the pool.

Mom and Dad told me I was a fuck up at the hospital. *Just like the Becketts,* they added. Said I deserved trailer trash like Erica.

Everything I thought I knew changed when they said that. What I believed to be subtle and understandable concern about their kids hanging out around Erica's crazy aunt flipped.

They weren't worried about our safety but our reputation. And we played right along with the words of our parents. Felix's parents were in on it, and Jared just followed along with us when we agreed maybe we should cut ties when she moved.

I hate myself and my reasoning to this day. *My reputation mattered more to me than the girl I viewed as my best friend.* But she was more than that.

At eighteen years old, I made a selfish choice. For eleven years I've regretted letting Erica Bennett go. Not one moment has gone by where the self-loathing doesn't try to drag me to hell.

Erica has haunted me since the moment we all agreed to ghost her. Seeing her look down on me like I'm nothing but dirt beneath her shoe is far more painful than I ever thought possible.

"Erica..."

The woman before me with bright blue hair and a *fuck me* bra berates me for my slip of the tongue.

She *just* fucking told Felix her name is Blue. *Why am I such a fuck up?* Erica is gone. I've had this said to me so many times in the past twenty-four hours since Jared and Declan came home looking as if they'd seen a ghost.

Blue shreds me with her words, making my heart ache with sorrow. I've never stopped beating myself up for cutting her out of my life, but I also never reached out once I realized how my parents manipulated us away from *trailer trash.* I listened to their previous advice to let the past stay in the past.

It was the easy road...Because I knew if I called her up, I'd have to atone for the part I played in our group abandonment of the sweet girl we all loved.

Jared, Declan, and Felix were there that day at the hospital, too. They heard everything. And still, like a bunch of childish bastards, we chose not to find Erica again.

I'm beginning to wonder if that was the right call now.

"Petal..." I croak, searching for the high schooler I once knew who always smiled and laughed. Erica may no longer exist, but my petal is still in there somewhere.

Right?

Wrong.

"We don't serve assholes. Get out."

Ouch. I would rather be called an asshole than hear her call us cruel like Jared and Dec said she did. Still, it fucking sucks, and it's another reminder of how she feels about us now.

Just as I'm about to protest our dismissal, a douchebag squeezes in beside Felix. "Blue, babe!"

In unison, the four of us stiffen. Even *Blue* fucking stiffens which doesn't sit right with me. She may not want our attention, but she clearly doesn't want this frat boy's attention either. What is he, twenty? Zero facial hair and high cheekbones aim right at Eri—*Blue*—completely ignoring the other bartender who starts making his drink. *Dale...Stupid name.*

"Blue, how 'bout that shot tonight, hmm?"

Christ, how drunk is this kid?

Blue's eyebrows twitch and her nose scrunches a little, yet she still plays nice. "Not tonight. We're too busy."

What bordered on disrespect turns into complete hostility. "Seriously? Just one shot. You fucking owe me, bitch."

My eyes snap from Blue's shocked face just in time to see Felix grab the guy by his throat. "What the *fuck* did you just say to her?!" Felix snarls, spinning Dale around. The bang of Dale's back on the edge of the bar would make me cringe in any other circumstance, but I'm fucking furious.

Jared backs up, giving Felix space to threaten Dale.

Meanwhile Declan, my younger brother, rushes toward Felix.

"Fuck!" I hiss and lunge for my brother. "Dec, don't get in the middle!"

My fingers brush the back of Declan's shirt, but I'm too late to save him from the violence. We all know not to get between Felix and his prey when he gets like this.

The four of us have the same demons, but the way we fight them is very different. Felix is the most volatile version.

Declan's worry about Felix blinds him. My brother grabs hold of Felix's arms to pull him off of Dale, but that one tug gives the frat boy the opening he needs to punch Declan right in the goddamn mouth.

"HEY!" Blue screams, drawing our attention as other people shout around us. Like a raging bull, Blue swings a big ass water bottle through the air, only for it to bang on the bar top when Dale moves out of the way.

"Holy fucking shit!" the dead man bellows. "Crazy fucking bitch! I'm gonna—"

"Get arrested, you son of a bitch!" another man says, snatching Dale's arms and dragging him through the crowd.

Plenty of cursing continues around us, but I only hear Declan's mumbled sound of pain.

"Let me see." When I pull his hand from his mouth, I'm not shocked at how much blood comes pouring out. "Tooth?" I ask, already searching for some clean napkins.

He nods, but his attention is on Felix arguing with a security guy. My friend is probably demanding he gets his own chunk of Dale's flesh. Unfortunately, that's not how the real world works.

"Here!" A hand thrusts into my line of sight holding a washcloth with what I assume is ice bundled in it. "Ice makes a great weapon too, but it's usually best for swelling."

The other two bartenders laugh, and Declan sputters out blood.

Startled by that statement, I look at the woman who used to be my girl. "Explain why you know that while I help Dec."

What opening I just had dissolves behind shuttered blue eyes. "No. Take this and get out."

With that, she drops the offering on the boozy bar, and stomps away to help some girls requesting her attention. They're all smiles and hugs, as if watching Blue swinging a steel fucking weapon around is normal.

Ice is a good weapon?

What in the hell happened to Erica?

Thirteen

BLUE

I'm debating moving out of state. If I had known this was going to happen a few months ago when my aunt ditched me and Violet, I would have moved across the country.

I don't want anything to do with the four fuckfaces who think they reserve the right to defend me. Honestly, I need protection from *them*.

Felix and his brooding, sexual, strong presence. Declan with his pushy, reckless attention. Confused and gentle Jared. Roman's puppy dog eyes and obvious pain.

They all batter against the walls I've built around the memories of them. I had to spend the day at home yesterday, ignoring everyone and everything—not Violet of course—to force my head back on straight.

I allowed myself to feel the pain of their actions *again*.

Just because Felix threw Dale around on Monday and Declan got hurt doesn't mean they're worth thawing my heart for. Never again will they be worth my vulnerability.

I can't afford to go there with anyone. I'm busy trying to build the life I want, while giving Violet everything I can. My sweet, sassy girl should never have had to grow up the way she did.

I'm ignoring the fact that the same could be said about me.

It's easier to focus on other people's pain than my own. Which is why I'm currently at the liquor store searching for Dakota's favorite wine. She broke up with her boyfriend this morning, so it's all hands on deck to mend our friend's broken heart.

Bethany's been cooking all morning, and Janine is already at Beth's house with ice cream. *Cliché?* You bet your ass. What better reason is there to eat yummy shit and give in to the tears adults have to force down every day than a breakup?

Blowing out a breath when I find the Chardonnay, I grab one. We'll need at least two and a bottle of vodka maybe. Shit, it's a Wednesday, though. Fuck it.

"Erica!"

"AH!" I startle. My twisted wrist spasms, making me drop the bottle. *CRASH!* "Shit!"

The wine shatters at my feet, and angry tears spring to my eyes. Manly exclamations of shock and apologies only serve to thicken the ball of frustration in my throat.

Why is he HERE?!

My God, why can't I catch a break? Seeing them so frequently in such a short amount of time is weakening me. I hate this. I hate *them!*

Every time I see one of their faces or hear their voices, I remember all the nights I cried myself to sleep. Fear and sorrow were the only things keeping me warm. At seventeen, I was left alone in a world where older men shoved me around, threatened to steal my panties, and did their best to sneak into my bedroom at night.

With the short amount of time I've had to process their presence in my city, I've come to realize Jared, Declan, Roman, and Felix are a trigger. They're the embodiment of loneliness and fear for me.

"Erica? Shit, are you okay?"

Why is it that Jared's words hurt more than the silence he subjected me to back then?

That's not my name.

"Erica, look at me," Jared pleads as the whooshing in my ears begins to lessen.

That's not my fucking name.

"Christ, Erica, you're scaring me!"

Four times is enough. Jared just sent me over the motherfucking edge. "That's not my name!"

With my hands fisted at my sides, I refuse to look at the asshole who's making a hard day even harder. I'd rather look at spilled wine and shattered pieces of glass than at his face.

He may be an incredibly handsome man, but all his looks do for me is light a spark of hostility.

Silence lingers heavily until it's broken by the crunch of glass. "Blue...I'm sorry. Let's just get you out of the glass."

"I'll get a broom," someone informs us from down the aisle.

Two dark hands enter my line of sight, blocking the carnage beneath me. All I can picture when I look down at the broken bottle is how much it resembles what the four of them did to me.

"Go away," I whisper, fighting like hell to keep my voice from wobbling.

Annoyance boils in my gut. Not just with Jared but with myself. I'm a badass, and I know my fucking worth. Why am I still a blubbering mess when it comes to these guys eleven years later?

"Bee, you're in little sandals." His voice is strained. "Let me help you."

I can't help the snort that comes out of me. *The audacity.* At least his dumbass comment snaps me out of whatever standoff I had going on with the broken wine bottle. Without much fanfare, I push his warm hands aside and grab two bottles.

"Bee, don't," Jared warns in a rush as I tiptoe through the shards. "Fucking hell, woman."

Ignoring him and the guy rushing around us to sweep up the hazard, I head for the registers. Jared's still begging me to talk to him, to *look* at him, but I don't. I won't.

Today is about *Dakota's* broken heart. Not mine. I won't let this asshole take more from me right now, not when I have to give myself to my best friend. Jared can take his useless help and his crappy nickname and shove it right up his fucking ass.

Barely restraining my middle finger from flipping

Jared off once I hop in my car, I drive away without looking back. *That's a lie*...My sad little heart forces me to glance in my rearview mirror. I knew it was a bad idea, and now I'm suffering with an ache in my chest all the way to Bethany's cute townhome where Dakota and she had a sleepover last night.

Pulling around back, I find a spot to park. Her parking is weird since it's on the edge of downtown Chicago. The deep breath I take does a decent job of cleansing my negative energy. At least that's what I'm telling myself. If I can't shake Jared off, I'll just twist my feelings and aim them at Dakota's cheating ex.

Fucker had the hottest, funniest woman...*Idiot*.

With my fanny pack slung over my shoulder and the brown paper bag of wine, I hop out of my car. I step back a bit, and hit the lock button, then do it three more times just to be sure it actually locked.

Car gets broken into one time and the paranoia follows me years later. My new vibrator got stolen though, so can anyone blame me for quadruple checking it's actually locked?

It turns out the answer is *yes* someone *can* blame and judge me. Not just anyone, either.

"You going to hit the button again or do you think you got it this time?"

Jared.

Fourteen

FELIX

T he way our townhouse is set up is a bit odd. The street is basically our front yard, and the five backyards are gorgeous with gardens, patios, and sidewalks separating the spaces.

The parking situation makes my room incredibly annoying. Don't get me wrong, I think our place is beautiful and far enough away from the hustle and bustle of downtown that I'm not terrified of a break-in. But that doesn't mean everyone else isn't worried.

Beep beep.

Beep beep.

Just when I think they'll stop locking their fucking car...

Beep beep.

I swear to fuck—

Beep beep.

I'm up and out of my desk chair without further thought. It doesn't cross my mind that a child might be playing with some keys. All I'm aware of is my annoyance as I storm through the house and out the back sliding glass door.

I can't see much through the line of trees, but I hear raised voices. Stomping along the path between yards, I catch a glimpse of...*Jared?*

"I'm not stalking you, Blue! I live here."

Blue?

"Bullshit!" Aaaand there she is, my reason for being on such a short fucking fuse this week. Her bright blue hair is up in a messy bun, she has no makeup on, and her biker shorts are almost completely covered with a big band T-shirt.

Whose fucking shirt is that?

"Good afternoon, Blue," I greet, my voice thick with untamed desire and frustration.

I wish I could convince myself that the way she stiffens when she hears me is because of excitement. *It's not.* Erica, as a teenager, would have squealed and run into my arms if I had surprised her. Because I didn't go to school with the rest of them, my presence was always met with happiness back then.

She most definitely is *not* happy now.

"So it's true, then?" Blue's voice is cold and sounds closer to a mental breakdown with each word.

"That we live here? Yeah. Almost a month now."

A wave of panic flickers through her gaze, making me tense. *Did I say something wrong?* Blue's arms tighten around a large paper bag.

Jared curses under his breath and offers Blue the smaller, more obvious liquor store paper bag. "Here, Bee. I bought you another one as some kind of peace offering for the next time I saw you." Her eyes narrow at my friend. Jared sighs and drags a hand through his short dark hair. "I didn't *know*. Stop looking at me like that."

Blue's gaze darts between us, and continuously skitters to the row of houses behind me. "Wait. Do you live here?" I ask, thinking I've figured out why she's acting like this is the end of the world.

"Thankfully, no," she sneers and lifts her chin in obvious defiance. "Seems like they just let *anyone* live here."

"Blue!" a feminine voice shouts. "Get your ass in here! The snacks aren't working. It's time for the booze!"

I make the mistake of looking behind me to see which neighbor knows Blue, but the damn trees and line of perfect bushes block my view. A slight breeze, one that I'm becoming well acquainted with, breezes past my arm. Blue rushes past me, but unlike like the time in the lounge, my pants aren't around my knees, and she doesn't have a door to slam in my face.

"Er—Blue wait!" Fuck, it's hard thinking of her as anything other than the girl we once knew. Rushing forward, I grab her elbow. Immediately, I regret it.

"Shit!" Blue hisses, fumbling with the bag I just jostled. But she's too late to right my wrong.

With her left elbow in my arm, the bottle of wine that was secured on that side in the bag goes crashing to the ground. I'm already apologizing and feeling like a fucking asshole, but Blue's not listening.

Yanking out of my hold, she whirls around on me

and absolutely *screams*. "DON'T TOUCH ME! DON'T LOOK AT ME! LEAVE ME ALONE!"

Chest heaving, with her fingers white-knuckling the remaining bottle of wine, Blue hits her breaking point. My stomach drops at the clear distrust in her sparkling blue eyes, and my heart shatters when they fill with tears. What I thought was enough guilt to last a lifetime doubles. Triples. Multiplies until I can't think straight when she begs with moisture coating her cheeks.

"Please," Blue whispers, stepping back onto pieces of glass. "*Please.*" Then she's rushing away with soft, hiccupping sobs as her soundtrack.

"Fucking hell," Jared mutters, sounding pained as he moves to stand next to me.

I nod. "Yeah."

I'd like to say my tone comes out strong and annoyed still, but that would be a horrible lie. I sound like the love of my life just kicked me in the balls and told me to go to hell. Actually, I'd rather that had happened. Maybe the pain in my heart would hurt less if my groin got the brunt of her anger.

But that's just it, isn't it? This isn't just about *anger*. There's so much more beneath that. *Hurt, sadness, contempt*—to name a few. And maybe I'm wrong about a few of those. One thing's for certain, we hurt our girl when we ghosted her. In more ways than we realize.

"You know what's funny?"

Jared's question startles me out of my anguished pondering. "What could possibly be funny right now?"

"First, I also made her drop a bottle of wine twenty

minutes ago. And second, we don't have a broom to clean this up."

My head tips back on a resigned sigh. "We're such fucking idiots."

"Yeah," Jared agrees and slams a hand down on my shoulder. "But I have a spare bottle of that exact wine, and I'm sure her friends have something we can sweep this up with."

Seeing the brown bag for what it is—a ticket in to see Blue again—I lunge for it, but Jared laughs and rushes away to find our girl.

Our girl? Is that even possible anymore?

I really fucking hope so.

Fifteen

BLUE

Five minutes is all it took for me to escape the worried looks of my friends. Their questions were almost as bad, but the concern in their eyes was too much for me.

I'm fine. *I'm fucking fine.*

Plus, we're here for Dakota. Not me. And I don't need them to be here for me anyway. I'm just fine.

My shaky breaths beg to differ though, as do my trembling fingers. I'll be okay; I just need to keep reminding myself of that for a while.

"God," I huff and splash my red cheeks. I'm acting like a fool around the guys. The easy way they reach for me and touch me is uncalled for. They don't know the number of times I've been grabbed and pushed around without consent.

What gives them the right to my attention and skin?! *They* broke *me*. Not the other around.

Once upon a time, I would bask in their physical

affection and demanding presence. Now it sends me right into fight-or-flight mode.

When it comes to the four of them, I want to fight. Throwing punches and kicks seems like a great stress reliever, but I keep fucking it up. Every time they're near, I want to cry, scream, and just disappear. What did I do to deserve their torment all over again?

Sure, they might not be physically hurting me, but Jesus Christ, the emotional pain of eleven years slams against my ribcage when they're around. Even when I'm thinking about them.

Their touch not only triggers me, but *burns* me. I very clearly don't want anything to do with them, yet their determination to connect is making everything worse.

Patting my cheeks dry on Bethany's hand towel, I spiral in my thoughts until numbness settles over my heart and mind like a hug. *Bless.* Sometimes over-thinking is exactly what shuts my brain off. *Eventually.*

Which is why, when the doorbell rings as I'm exiting the bathroom, I don't think much of it. Being the closest to the entryway, I pivot and tighten my messy bun.

I'll probably need to go back to the liquor store, which will need to happen before I start drinking. *Maybe some White Claws would be—*

My easy planning sputters out when I open the door. The numbness that weighs nicely on my conscience wavers in the face of the four men who have sent me into more panic-attacks in a short week than I've had in a year.

"Hi, Bee." Jared waves at me with a bottle of wine. *I wouldn't need to buy another one if he's offering.*

Declan shuffles, looking quite yummy in his gray sweatpants and black tank top. I trail my gaze over him with indifference even as my adrenaline rises. In his hand looks to be a plastic Tupperware.

He must notice my frown because he answers my unspoken question. "Oh. Your friend, Bethany—I think —gave us cookies when we moved in. I'm returning her dish because that's what people do?"

God fucking damn it, my lips twitch. That one glimpse into who Declan's grown up to be reminds me of him as a teenager.

Schooling my features, I raise a brow when I notice Roman clutching what I think is the lid for the bowl.

"I—" Roman clears his throat, looking embarrassed and tired? "I'm returning the lid."

I would laugh if I didn't think it would open doors that need to stay firmly fucking locked. Like the door I'm holding open. I really should slam it in their faces, but they have Beth's stuff. And wine.

Dismissing the Ledger brothers and Jared, I find Felix off to the side with empty hands. "Uh," he hesitates and shifts, looking uncertain which seems extremely out of character for him. "I need to borrow a broom and dustpan."

A loud laugh behind me makes me jump. Glaring over my shoulder, I spot Janine who's red in the face beside Beth and Dakota who are clearly biting their tongues, and beg them to go away.

They don't, of course.

"Who doesn't have a broom?" Bethany wonders out loud, cocking her head a little.

"Only necessities came with us during our move," Felix answers matter-of-factly.

"Blue..." Jared murmurs, holding out the bottle of wine. "Please take it."

I don't so much as sigh as I pull it from his large grip. Indifference will make them go away, I'm sure of it. They're like children, hoping for any kind of reaction because it means you're paying attention.

Dakota steps forward, then takes the lid and bowl from Declan and Roman. I figure we're about ready to shut the door on them, but she opens her goddamn mouth. "How do you guys know Blue?"

Fucking fuckity fuck.

Hurt flashes across all four of their handsome faces. I wonder what they hope my friends know.

"High school," I grit out while avoiding eye contact with all seven of them. This bottle of wine can't be popped open fast enough.

"Really?" Janine drawls with one eyebrow raised at me. *Is she putting the pieces together?*

"We had a falling out," I add, really hoping it's enough. It's the most basic form of the truth.

"A falling out..." Felix rumbles.

Silence.

Then Bethany mutters something about the broom. Hopefully she'll be back soon so we can send them on their way. Guilt blossoms in my belly, making me feel nauseous.

I don't hold much guilt in my life. I've done the best

I could for myself and for Violet. Do I wish I could have given her a better upbringing? Abso-fucking-lutely. But I was eighteen years old with no preparation for raising a little girl.

I've done a great job for us. A lot of sadness and anger haunts me, but not guilt.

Until now.

Bethany hands over a broom to Felix who's frowning at me. I close the door without another word. I have a lot of explaining to do, but I'm not at all ready to face my best friends.

With the guys gone and my girls watching me with a mix of confusion and hurt, I feel the tears come back. "Let me get some wineglasses first, please."

My friends know everything about my adult life. Eighteen and over they're aware of. My trauma, the lack of food and clothes, all the horrible fuckwits my aunt subjected me to...They know it all.

But the four men who just left? My best friends have never heard of Roman, Felix, Declan, and Jared. What they know is moving away from my friends and school during sophomore year was really hard, and I lost a lot of support.

It was a door I didn't want opened ever again.

But I busted that right the fuck down when I literally opened Beth's front door.

I need some wine to finally be honest with my girl friends. Thankfully, V and I are getting out of town for a week so I can run away from the bomb I'm about to drop on them.

I'm the worst.

"You're shitting me! I'm going to kill them. I'll go over there and cut their ears off one by one then toss them down the garbage disposal!"

Wide-eyed, Janine, Dakota, and I stare at Bethany. Sweet, kind, Bethany. "Beth, it's okay," I coo, scared that I broke my friend.

Blonde ringlets frame her rosy cheeks making her look slightly feral. "No, Blue. It's not okay. They were your best friends and gave you no reason for why they ghosted you. They're pieces of childish shit."

"Beth—"

"You were punched, pushed down the stairs, locked out of the house, starved, raised a child, drug from place to place, and violated *twice*!"

Shit. "I wasn't vio—"

"YES YOU WERE!" Bethany screams, her own trauma expanding and making her hyperventilate. "Twice that man snuck into your bedroom and pulled the blankets off of you, Blue. He *touched* you. I don't care that he only got as far as lifting your shirt both times before you woke up, *you were violated*!"

I might be sick. The easy thing to do right now would be to ask one of the other girls to comfort Bethany and hide in the bathroom again while I cry. But I don't because it's important to acknowledge the shit I endured.

Plus, my issues made one of my best friends cry.

On my hands and knees, I crawl to my bestie and snuggle into her side. I know she's reliving her own past as we dredge mine up again, and hers, in my opinion, is far worse than mine. Yet she turned out to be the purest soul I've ever met.

Bethany sniffles and lays her head on top of mine. "They *knew* your home life was bad, Blue. How could they leave you like that?"

"I don't know..." Her question is one I've asked myself countless times, yet I still don't know the answer. I'm not sure if I ever will, but until I do, I'm living with assumptions.

And you know what they say...*When you assume, you make an ass out of you and me.*

Sixteen

DECLAN

Running a café for my parents wasn't something I thought I'd be doing when I grew up. It is lucky, though.

Mom and Dad retired last year, and their gift to me was their Chicago location. Did I want it? No. I'd rather find my own interests instead of staying in the family company.

But I said yes because I've never told my parents no. After the incident when I went off to college to get a business degree, our relationship has been strained. Their truth finally came out about why they urged us away from Erica, and I could never look at them the same.

Saying no and actively going against what they want is still incredibly hard to do. I know if they find out we're trying to befriend Erica again, they'll have a hissy fit and probably disown us.

Would I even care at this point? I'm not sure, but I would give them back the store. Thankfully I'm not the manager, but even as the owner my goal is to still be involved.

I've spent the last week studying our numbers and employee list. Next on my agenda is to meet everyone, host some meetings with the supervisors and staff. It feels weird not to be involved in my store, plus it gets me away from Felix.

I've been avoiding him as much as possible since we went to our neighbor's house last week with the Tupperware and wine bottle. It's been six days since any of us have seen Blue, and I'm feeling mighty itchy.

After pestering Bethany, Blue's friend and our neighbor, we found out she's on a road trip with Violet. Just the mention of Blue's daughter makes me see red. *Where the fuck is the baby daddy?*

"Hey man," Felix greets sleepily as he ambles toward the coffee machine.

Zoning out on his bare, muscled back, I sink into my annoyance. *Why the fuck is he up so early?* The way he calls me *man* upsets me. Maybe Jared has a point. If I tell Felix about my feelings and the raging boner I always have for him, maybe he'd finally *notice*.

I'm friendzoned, and it's been getting to me these past few months. Especially now that we have Erica back in our lives, albeit coincidental and forced, everything feels heightened.

My guilt, which once only hindered my mental state, is now eating me alive. Blue would hardly look at me when I was right there, and when she did, the pain in her sparkly blue eyes twisted the knife in my heart.

"You okay, bro?"

If I wasn't pissed a second ago, I most definitely am now. *Bro. Just twist the knife harder, asshole.* Slamming back the last of my coffee, I let the bitterness sink into my psyche.

"I don't know, Felix. Do I look fucking *fine* to you?!"

Abs point right at me, and dirty blond eyebrows slam down. "Jesus. What the fuck is your problem?"

Before I can cool myself down, I snarl, "You!" Snatching my keys off the counter, I storm out of the house and stomp to my car.

"Fucking dick, ruining my mood on my first day." My white-knuckled grip on the steering wheel calms me ever so slightly. The only thing I can control in my life is my driving, so I might as well do it right.

As I'm ending the drive to the café in downtown Chicago, the scene I made in the kitchen starts flickering in my mind. Now that I've been able to take a breath and separate myself from *one* of the people causing me heartache, I realize how impulsive and childish I acted.

All that realization does is annoy the shit out of me. I'm aware of my toxic tendencies, now what the hell do I do with them?

Parked in the back employee lot, I lock my car then lock it again. *Can't be too careful.* With my keys in the front pocket of my black jeans, I check my buttons on my shirt. Casual but respectable.

Just when I think I have myself under control, I step through the front door of Butter and Bloom and find Blue Bennett waiting at the pickup spot.

"Where's Violet?" *Why did that come out accusatory?*

My way of greeting the girl who never hurt so much as a fly is borderline asking for a punch in the face.

Blue jolts, looking up from her phone. "What?"

I glance at her ring finger on both hands. "No ring. Baby daddy a piece of shit, huh?"

"What the fuck are you talking about, Declan?" Blue looks completely shocked and lost. I don't blame her. Nor can I blame Felix for my foul mood.

I'm having an out-of-body experience. I *know* I should stop and apologize, but can't. "Your kid, Violet. Her daddy didn't marry you, huh?"

Fuck.

I watch every single change in Blue's demeanor. As if in slow motion, her furrowed brows shift into a flat line like my heart tries to do. Her lips purse and her sharp jaw flexes.

Shit. Shit. Shit.

"BB!" a barista calls out. My attention tracks Blue as she smiles at the young girl behind the counter. They chat for a few seconds in hushed voices, but it ends with both Blue and my staff member nodding.

Blue blows the barista a kiss and steps away with her iced coffee. I think she's about to walk right by me without a second thought, but she stops at the last second.

What she says next absolutely fucking *ruins* me. "Violet's father is dead."

Then she's gone. She's a breeze that passes by me and leaves so much fucking guilt in her wake.

Violet's dad is dead?! Blue's a single mom? Jesus, are they doing okay? I mean, it *seems* like Blue's doing all right for herself. She can afford my overpriced coffee and take Violet on weeklong trips. Alone, though?

"Fuck!" I hiss, rubbing a hand down my face. *What the hell is wrong with me?* I'm not even quite sure what I was accusing her of. I was angry she left for a week and pissed at Felix for not noticing how much I love him.

The common denominator in both of those issues is me and my lack of productive communication.

I open my eyes at the realization that I need to have some serious conversations, only to find out there are even *more* tough talks I should add on as well. Three of my employees and my manager are glaring at me.

Worst first impression of all time.

Seventeen

BLUE

I'm fuming. Absolutely *fuming*.

Declan was always a bit of an ass in high school, but that was fucked up. Who is he to ask about Violet's dad? As far as I'm concerned, Violet is none of his business. Especially not Carl.

Holy shit. I'm shaking. Completely baffled, I stomp off the elevator.

V and I had an amazing road trip this past week. Of course I'm tired, but I've felt wonderfully sore and much lighter since we got home last night. I let go of everything and just spent time with my girl.

Today's my only day off before work tomorrow, so I woke up at the ass crack of dawn because V is wild. When I couldn't hang anymore, I left to get a latte at my favorite coffee shop in our building.

Butter and Bloom was definitely a large part of why I chose to live *here*. Who wouldn't see a coffee shop below their apartment and think *fuck yes, I need that in my life.*

I'm still pissed off after about ten minutes of sitting on my couch with my latte. Damn Declan for ruining my cozy morning. Flipping my Kindle closed, I jump up and cue some *Linkin Park* through my speakers.

Angry music is just what I need while I clean some of this nasty energy out of me. Maybe it's counterproductive, but I don't care.

My throat thickens with bubbling emotion as I scream the lyrics to *Emptiness Machine*. "I let you cut me open just to watch me bleed! Gave up who I am for who you wanted me to be!"

That won't be me. I won't allow them to steal who I am ever again! The burn in my forearms doesn't matter, nor do I feel it as I soak in the words of one of my favorite bands.

Fire lights my vocal cords as I completely dive into a particularly *angry* song. "Let me out, set me free!" "Casualty" by Linkin Park fuels my rage, not only at the four men who broke my heart, but at myself for still being upset about it. "I won't be your casualty!"

Over and over again, I scream those lyrics until the crack in my soul completely shatters. The rag in my shaking hands flies into the washing machine with a *thud*. I slam the lid down with a much more satisfying *bang*.

I won't be their casualty. They've been turning me into someone I don't recognize. At the age of eighteen, I had to learn to manage my emotions while balancing adult life and fun to take care of Violet.

Allowing them to derail me and my mental health is

not an option. "I'm not their casualty." Maybe eleven years ago I was, but not anymore.

The past is in the past.

It has to stay there so it doesn't blind me to my promising future.

Smiling, I close Violet's door after checking on her. She's had a long two weeks and didn't rest much today. My girl is full of energy.

With silent feet, I tiptoe back to the living room where a glass of wine awaits me. On nights like these, when it's past nine on a Wednesday and the city is quieter, I feel like I belong for once.

Life in Chicago has been a dream. I've found my people, and get along with everyone well enough. Unless they're awful and I have to threaten them with my steel water bottle.

My ass hits the cushions, and a relieved sigh escapes me. Working nights doesn't allow me much relaxation time after the world goes to sleep. It's nice.

I've exorcized my demons through cleaning and screaming, now I'm ready to jump back into my usual schedule.

If I could, I would choose to travel with Violet every day of my life. We would have a home base, of course, but we'd always be on the road. Neither of us are home-bodies, constantly wanting to do stuff and be...more.

Our childhoods were stifled, and it shows.

Draining the last sip of my wine, I let my head fall on the cushion and attempt to clear my mind. I've almost accomplished my goal when my phone buzzes on the armrest beside me.

Not thinking much of it, I grab the device and lift it above my face so I can keep relaxing. Tapping the screen, I squint against the bright light. Everything in me freezes, and the unsolicited gasp makes me choke.

My phone slips from my fingers, cracking me in the eyebrow. I can't quite catch a breath as I scramble for it, just to prove to myself that I'm not crazy.

I'm not crazy.

Roman texted me.

Roman 🖤
June 18th, 2025

> Roman 🖤: Please don't dismiss this. Please, Blue. I need to see you. It's important.

I feel sick. *Why didn't I change his name in my phone?* It's been eleven years, so I don't have the proof of Roman ghosting me anymore, but I still feel that pain as if it were yesterday.

Something about the kind of betrayal I went through has really stuck with me. That kind of breach of trust lingers.

They were my friends, my family. Their parents might have watched me with suspicion but they never kicked me to the curb. The boys loved me. Or so I thought.

I'm debating how to respond when his chat bubble appears and disappears. It happens a few times before his next message comes in, sealing my approach.

> Roman 🖤: You have every right to ignore this and I'm sorry for that. For so so many things, Blue.

> Me: Meet me at Butter and Bloom at eight tomorrow morning.

> Roman 🖤: I'll be there. Thank you.

Someone would ask me *why*? Why in the hell would I agree to get a coffee with one fourth of my problems?

I refuse to be their casualty anymore. Admitting I've been allowing them to alter my life was difficult, but it was true. The hurt they caused was brought right back to the surface with their presence in Chicago, and literally everywhere I go.

It's time I face this head-on and close that chapter of my life.

Eighteen

ROMAN

I 've been shaking since I texted Blue last night. There are many reasons I look like I'm a millisecond from passing out.

One being that Blue actually agreed to see me. I couldn't believe it, then again, she was always the heart of our little group. She would drop anything for us faster than we dropped her.

Second, I manipulated her. I intentionally made it seem like something was wrong because I knew she was still the tenderhearted teenager I met in high school.

Thirdly, I lied to the guys and one hundred percent withheld important information about Blue. All four of us are sitting around a table at Declan's café, yet I'm the only one who knows the real reason.

Nobody knows what I have in store this morning. Honestly, I'm not even quite sure what I have planned. I'm grasping at straws here. It's almost July. We've been here for like four weeks, and still we haven't made any progress with Blue.

Thankfully, nobody had to skip work today, except Declan, but he was already sitting at the wooden table with a stack of papers anyway. I wonder if Blue knows he owns this café.

Jared doesn't start working at the high school for a while yet. With it being summer, he had a decent break from being a math teacher, but I know he plans to get a head start on the curriculum for his first year there.

Felix starts his new job tonight and I seriously cannot *wait* to hear how it goes. I might stop by and await the explosion that is bound to happen.

I still haven't figured out how I'll earn money. My passions are pretty limited, but I have some skills. I'm not interested in business like my younger brother and Felix. Math and school aren't my jam, but I can lift weights and help my friends gain some muscle.

Maybe I'll look into personal training opportunities. I did that for a bit right out of high school but fell in line with my parents' pressure to get a degree.

"Hey, sorry." Declan sighs, collapsing into a wooden chair next to me. "I'm trying to understand their organization in the backroom, and it's not computing in my head."

Felix crosses his arms and leans back. "Why do you need to understand it? If it works for your staff, why does it matter?"

A flash of *something* flashes through Declan's eyes, and I can't help but wonder about my brother's reactions to Felix lately. "Because I own this place, and I should know how my people work. I'm not looking to change it. I'm not a dick."

"I never said you were," Felix replies smoothly.

"Well, if Felix won't say it..." a soft, angry, and feminine tone says. I stiffen, knowing that voice anywhere. "I will. You're a dick, Declan."

Blue's floral scent wraps around me as she steps closer. No force in the world could stop me from dragging my gaze up her gorgeous body. Beside my right shoulder, Blue's dressed in cotton red shorts and a baggy white T-shirt tied in a knot over her belly button.

My dick takes notice immediately and my mouth waters. Holy shit. *Has she been walking around Chicago like this?* I can't even tell if she's wearing a bra.

"So are you Roman," she snaps, pulling me out of my lust-induced haze. I mean, my God, she's a fucking goddess. She's so close I could lick her belly button. "What is this? Some kind of intervention? Trick Blue into hanging out so we can show her we're not all bad?"

I feel the tension rise around the table making my heart thunder in my chest. Christ, I never used to have so many issues. In college with Felix, I was the life of the party. Since my parents dropped their toxic bomb, I haven't been able to pull myself out of this suffocating pit of depression.

There is no oxygen to give life to the fun, outgoing Roman I used to be. He's just lying there in a patch of wet dirt wondering how the hell he was so gullible and selfish to throw away this beautiful flower.

"Petal..."

Crystal blue eyes sharpen on mine. "Don't call me

that. Your pretty flower is nothing but wilted petals, Roman."

My gut sinks. She can't mean that. The Erica I knew was bubbly and outgoing. I still see that in her. She's still my Petal.

But if I believe the old me is at the bottom of a moldy pit, why is it so hard to believe Blue when she tells me past Erica is dead? Is she really nothing more than a wilted flower?

Slowly, I begin to nod. "Okay, Blue. I hear you..."

She rolls her eyes. "Sure you do. So what is this? What's so important you dredged my number from the depths of your contact list after all this time?"

"Roman, you planned this?" Jared kicks my leg under the table, looking shocked and amused.

I nod, feeling guilty as hell even if he's excited.

Declan sucks in a breath and jumps up so fast his knees bang into the table. "Here. Please sit. Can I get you anything to eat or drink?"

Blue takes his seat easily and without hesitation, like she's claiming the treatment she's due. I'm applauding her in my head. She's become a strong woman in our absence. *Maybe this wasn't a good idea...*

"I—" Shit. What if we just make her life worse? Have we already? This feels like a step too far.

"Spit it out, Roman. Feel guilty for manipulating me later."

I seriously cannot express how happy I am to witness her strength. Whatever she went through didn't break her. *We* didn't break her.

I chance a look at the other guys who seem to be

waiting for me as well. Which makes sense since I brought us all together under the guise of half-truths and zero plans. *Fuck.*

"Please give us the chance to explain," I beg, my words feeling like knives crawling up my throat. What if after we explain, she still tells us to get lost?

I wouldn't blame her.

Blue moves her hair over her shoulder and cocks her head. "Explain what exactly? It feels like there are so many things." She glares at Declan who has found a new chair.

He sighs and scrubs a hand down his face. *Did something else happen?*

Felix catches on to my plan and leans forward. "Everything. Let us explain all of it."

Silence descends, and the nausea I've been struggling with since last night rises. I swear I'm about to throw up when a young woman with bright blonde hair in a high ponytail skips up to our table. She can't be older than twenty.

"Good morning," the newcomer drawls with a hand on her hip. She's slender and muscular like Blue, but a bit shorter. "Who are all of you?"

Jared looks taken aback, which I'm sure we all do. *Who is this woman?* "Uh. I'm Jared. How can we help you?"

"Ma?"

Who's Ma?

To my complete shock, Blue sighs. "This is Roman," she gestures to me, "Felix, and Declan."

"Owner of Butter and Bloom," Declan adds, sounding proud. *Good for him.*

Blue whips around to face him. "You're shitting me!"

"Nope." My brother grins.

"We live in the building. Is that how you all met?" the blonde questions, still flashing looks at Blue.

"You live here?" Jared's excitement over new information is contagious. Now we know where to find her.

"Yep!" Blondie chirps. "Oh, and I'm Violet, by the way. Blue's cousin."

Nineteen

BLUE

Declan chokes. Sputtering on his sip of coffee, he looks like a damn idiot who should have kept his mouth shut yesterday.

I'm not totally positive I know what he was insinuating when he was dissing my empty ring finger, but wow. Watching my cousin steal the wind beneath his wings is going down as one of my most favorite petty moments.

I can't hold my smirk in, but I'm not about to trauma dump with Violet watching. She's witnessed enough as is. "V, honey, I have some asses to kick. Meet you for dinner before my shift?"

Curiosity flashes in her eyes. Thankfully, she doesn't push the subject right now because she most definitely plans to later. "Sure, Ma." She blows me a kiss and skips away.

I wish I had half of her energy. She's probably going on a hike with her friends and making another livestream on one of her social media platforms. How she makes money off of videotaping herself doing random things is beyond me.

Whatever works for her. At least she can pay for her own adventures now.

"Why does she call you Ma?" Roman questions me softly with a warm nudge on my arm.

I jerk away and mask the move by taking a sip of my drink. Felix notices, but I ignore his intake of breath. "Because I raised her. Her dad died, and custody was transferred to my aunt when Violet was seven."

"How old were you?" Felix looks like he's ready to hunt down the key to unlock all of my answers.

I look him dead in his angry eyes so I can witness my truth spearing him in his fucking *loyalty*. "I had just turned eighteen. My bags were packed, and I used all the money I had to buy a one-way plane ticket from Tacoma to New Orleans. Then the doorbell rang."

"And then?" Jared looks a little slightly shaken up, yet he's still determined to know why my life took a turn.

I blink, then blink again, remembering those first few months when Violet kept asking for her dad and my aunt, *her mother*, would scoff and walk away. Still, to this day, I hurt for the little girl I took under my wing.

"Then I unpacked my bags, gave her my secret food stash and did my very best to be what she needed after losing her amazing father." *Shit, don't cry.*

"Bee—"

While clenching my right fist as tight as I can in my lap, I shake my head. "Don't, Jared." I'm annoyed and frayed. "I have to go—"

"No, please don't," Roman begs, grabbing my fist before I can protest.

I tug but pause when Felix's accusing tone assaults my vulnerable heart. "Why are you here, Blue? We're stupid enough to let Roman manipulate the situation to get us all together, but you saw us before approaching. Why stay?"

Observant motherfucker. "Doesn't matter," I huff.

"Like hell it doesn't," Felix snaps back, his dirty blond hair flopping over his eyebrow with aggravation.

Give me patience...

"Felix, I really don't think you've earned literally any kind of explanation from me." Silence. "Do you?"

"Clearly we did something to *earn* your attention today, Er—Fuck! Blue." Flustered is a good look on Felix. A few times now I've been the reason his perfect jaw clenches and his shoulders heave with big breaths.

Go me. Fuck him. Oh my god. That's my new motto.

"Are you even listening?" Felix growls, leaning forward as if to intimidate me.

"*Are you still here*?" I fire back, letting my sass flag fly.

"Listen—"

Declan grabs Felix's bicep to stop the bigger man from attacking me. *Not that he would, but damn does he look mad.* Watching both of them freeze and look at the place they're touching is definitely not something I saw coming.

Declan's face heats from his cheeks to his hairline. Then he gulps, and I swear on all chocolate that these guys are going to have something pretty fucking serious to talk about after this.

They've either fucked in the past or will very soon. Judging by Felix's shuddering breath and the way he leans closer to Declan, there's definitely something mutual going on there.

My stomach twists. *Jealousy—what a bitch.* It's clear as day they have a connection, which means I have only two to kick off my heels.

Jared clears his throat, making it obvious that he either knows something or felt their sexual tension too. I shit you not, the two horny bastards don't even twitch. Eyes locked, it's like the rest of the world doesn't exist.

Interesting. I bet I could slip away without anyone noticing.

Jared coughs *again*, and Roman...clueless fucking Roman asks if he needs a water.

The sound of Roman's voice is like a bomb going off if the two lovebirds' reaction is anything to go by. They jump away from one another. I can't help my laugh.

I almost laugh *too* hard. Holy shit, you know? Witnessing what I just did was wild. I'm choosing to ignore the horrible feeling of loss of something I didn't even realize I still wanted.

Eleven years later, so much anger and heartbreak, and yet I'm still a pathetic bitch. *Ugh, get me out of here.*

"So this has been great." I stand, dragging my plastic cup along the table as I do so. "But I'm ready to call time of death, aren't you?"

"What does *that* mean?" Declan demands, still red in the face.

I raise a brow, unable to stop myself from taunting the flustered man. *"That meeeeans,"* I take a sip of my beverage and gesture to our merry band of broken men, "this isn't happening. We aren't friends, and I got everything I needed today."

"Wait," Roman gasps. "I asked you to come so *we* could explain. Not you. You haven't heard anything about our side of the story."

Sadness fills me. While I could benefit from an explanation, I have a life to live, not a past to dwell on. "I only have so many blank pages, Rome. And I'm choosing to fill them with *Blue*. Erica's story ended a long time ago. I gave her a short chapter today because she needed it. I'm moving on. You should too."

I only have so many pages...I won't fill them with excuses that only serve to invalidate the pain I survived.

Twenty

FELIX

I pride myself on my control. Normally I would say *loyalty*, but we all know how that went down. Christ, what a mess.

My *control* is all I have left it feels like. If this were one of those werewolf books that Declan likes to read, then I would be the alpha. But what does it say about the alpha when he has literally no idea what happened this morning?!

I had no idea Roman was capable of such deception. None of us did—clearly because we thought his anxiety last night and into today was *normal*. The dickhead was *sweating* for twelve hours. Declan, Jared, and I shrugged it off and just went to breakfast with him.

That's not to say I'm mad Blue showed up. Okay, maybe a little. Had I known *why* the hell we were there, I could have prepared myself for it. We focused on Blue and Violet the entire time—which *yes please*—but she needs to hear our fucking reasons to...to what?

What do we want?

I'm spinning out of control, and I'm about one wayward hair away from losing my goddamn mind. My control over myself. Apparently, I can't control Blue who wants fuck all to do with us. And Declan? What the hell was that?!

Obviously I think D's attractive in a subjective way. He's the *pretty boy* of our family—I have eyes. But that has never meant my dick does too. Until yesterday. His skin on mine jolted me, and when our eyes clashed, my dick sprung to life.

I fooled around plenty in college, had a dick in my mouth, whatever. But this? That *connection* lit my insides on fire. My groin turned into molten lava, and my lungs had to fight to keep breathing.

Declan didn't seem as shocked as I was, which left me with so many fucking questions. Questions that have gone unanswered all damn day. He's avoided me since Blue left us speechless at the breakfast table.

How screwed up would it be for me to ask Jared about this? *Fuck it.* "Yo, Jared!"

It takes a minute, but soon he's bounding into my bedroom. "Sup?" He retracts his greeting as soon as he sees my facial expression. "No."

"I didn't say anything." *He definitely knows something.*

Jared shakes his head. "I'm not getting in the middle."

"Middle of what?"

"Between you and Declan."

I got him right where I want him. "What about me and Declan?"

"Declan needs to talk to you about it."

"Why does Declan need to bring it up?" *Come on, give me something here...*

"After two years, I think it's time he manned up. His crush on you—" Jared's brown eyes widen. "You motherfucker! That was manipulation."

It's easy to pull information out of Jared and Declan because they're slightly loose cannons. Their energy and impulsiveness work in my favor sometimes.

I don't feel guilty about it right now, though. I'm fucking reeling. Standing up from my bed with my shoes on now, I begin to pace. "He's had a crush on me for years? What the hell, Jared?! Why didn't anyone tell me?!"

He hesitates, but when I whirl around on him, he folds. I sound like I'm lashing out in anger, but my expression shows the hurt and fear I'm suddenly drowning in.

Jared sighs and runs a hand through his short ringlets. "I've been trying for a long time to get him to open up about it. He's had a lot longer to wrestle with this than you have, Felix."

Fuck, that's fair. "Who else knows?"

"Roman doesn't seem to know if that's what you're wondering, but..." he trails off and smirks.

"But what?" Annoyance is beginning to steal my patience. I want the information so I can track Declan down and talk about this. Because everything has changed. Our group dynamic will never be the same.

Jared huffs a laugh. "Blue knows."

"WHAT?! How the hell does Blue know before me?!" What in the actual hell is going on around here? I feel like I'm ten steps behind everyone else when I'm normally ahead.

He full on laughs and walks out of my bedroom. I have no choice but to follow him as he treks into the kitchen for what I'm assuming is his fifth snack of the day. "The *fuck me* eyes at breakfast were an obvious giveaway."

Roman slams the fridge door closed, scaring the shit out of us. "What *fuck me* eyes?"

Jared groans and crumples onto the island like a drama queen. "Declan and Felix. Into each other."

"What? No I'm not." It's a knee-jerk reaction to deny feelings for someone I've always thought of as a little brother. But my heart shrivels in response to my denial. *Am I into Declan?*

Roman's eyebrows are hidden beneath his shaggy black hair, and his mouth is open like he gasped while I made an ass of myself. Shit. *Shit.* What is the right thing to say to my best fucking friend after our other friend drops a bomb like that? What's the right answer? Actually, what's the fucking truth?!

"Rome—"

His usually sad, vulnerable gaze turns cold as he straightens. "I suggest..." Roman begins and walks until he's about to pass me. He stops and glares into my soul. "... that when you break my little brother's heart, you do it respectfully. Because I'd really hate to beat your ass."

Then he's gone, leaving his threat hanging in the air. *Break mine too?* What, like he'd kick me to the curb and unfriend me?

"Shit..." Jared murmurs, looking nervous.

Shit is right. Because literally the only place my heart feels mostly full is with these guys. My family. I can't lose them. But I have no idea how to navigate this. And now I have to go fuck up someone else's life too.

I don't even know where the hell D is, but I need to go to work. Everything is out of my control. Except being on time. "See you later," I mutter to Jared and leave because facing this issue isn't possible right now.

I have other shit to ruin.

Twenty-One
BLUE

S erpent's Kiss is *not* a hangout spot. We're a club meant for alcohol and dancing. There's rarely anyone at the bar for more than five minutes.

Declan got the alcohol part right. Or *wrong* however you want to look at it. I'm not sure where he found the stool he's sitting on. He's kept his slice of the bar clean by being slumped over on it.

He was already way too wasted to hold a conversation by the time I got here. My shift was later tonight, and the bartender I replaced a half hour ago warned me about the drunk guy in the corner before she left.

Low and behold, it's Declan.

I've ignored him as best as I can considering the hair on the back of my neck has been standing on end since I got here. Every time I glance over at him, his face is still in his arms. *Why does it feel like someone's watching me?*

"Should we check on him? You know, make sure he's alive?" Bethany worries beside me as we make a line of jack-and-cokes.

"He's fine."

"But," she glances at him again, "what if he's not?"

Declan is clearly not *fine*, but I'm sure he's alive. Spiraling maybe, but breathing, I bet. I could wake him and urge him to go home so I can have a peaceful shift. *Yeah, that sounds nice.*

Since I wasn't ready to explain the guys to Violet, I skipped having dinner with her. I'm slightly on edge still, so maybe getting him out of here will calm me down enough to zone out.

The perk of being a bartender, similar to that of a barista, is I can lose myself in making the drinks. My mind shuts off, and my body goes into autopilot mode.

Right now, I could really use that. My brain is exhausted. I can't stop scolding myself for sitting at that damn breakfast table with them this morning. I knew I'd get hurt, but it just wasn't the way I assumed.

Declan and Felix? I never saw that coming.

With a sigh, I put a finger up, asking the customers to give me a second. A few grumble, but I've heard much worse. Working in customer support requires a backbone. And a steel water bottle sometimes.

"Declan," I urge once I'm in front of his sleeping body. No response. I really don't want to touch him. "Declan." Still nothing. Cursing, I reach my hand out and shake his shoulder even though I'd rather yank on his dark hair. "Dec—"

"AH!" he startles, jumping back and knocking over a drink beside him.

"Shit!" I hiss, reaching for the glass, but I'm caught looking guilty by a large man who turns around looking ready to murder me. Declan is shoved behind the wall of muscle glaring down at me.

Hastily, I start sliding the ice cubes toward me so they don't spill on the angry guy. I'm too late. The side of his shirt is drenched.

"You fucking bitch!" the stranger slurs and snatches my right wrist. He proceeds to yank me across the bar top, slamming my hips into the hard edge.

I gasp as he shouts at me for ruining his white shirt. Dread and something akin to a post-traumatic stress response stab my consciousness over and over again.

So many times I was at the mercy of men bigger than me. I got through those times with nothing but motivation to be there for Violet. Circumstances are different now, though. She's older. An adult. V doesn't need me anymore.

In the face of an angry drunk, I realize just how tired of fighting I really am. What is it about me that screams *hurt me*?

I know how to defend myself, and I'm damn good at it. In the position this guy has me in, with my body bent forward and my toes straining to stay on the ground, I feel vulnerable and weak.

Again.

My hand being slammed into the hard surface snaps me out of my thoughts long enough for the panic to steal the breath from my lungs. Blood rushes through my ears in response to the blooming ache in my wrist and hand.

"Are you even listening, cunt?!" Spit hits my forehead like a cold shower. *This motherfucker.* I pull back, but he barely budges. There's shouting around me and more hands reaching for my arm as I run through all the self-defense techniques Levi has taught me over the years.

It turns out I don't need to rescue myself this time. And it's not my friends who save me either.

"GET YOUR HANDS OFF MY WOMAN!"

The rush of relief that cools my veins when I hear Felix's order is stronger than when the unwanted touch of this beast is ripped away.

Flying back, I almost miss the punch Felix lands on the asshole's nose. Thankfully, I get to see the blood splatter and security descending on my assailant before I fall right on my ass.

My tailbone screams in response, making me hiss out a pained breath as I tense to keep my head from snapping back too.

"Oh my god!" Bethany screeches, coming to kneel beside me.

The ground is wet. My right hand and wrist are throbbing along with the ache in my hip bones and ass. I groan, clutching my injured extremity to my shuddering chest.

"Shit shit shit! Are you okay!?" Janine looks scared which sets me even more on edge. She doesn't wait for my response before grabbing my elbow to pull me up. I follow, albeit reluctantly, because I'd rather not see all the stares right now.

Shit happens when you work in an environment like ours. It's not the first time I've gotten hurt on the job or been called names, and it won't be the last. Which is part of the reason why I'd rather manage security because if I were in charge, the bar would always be staffed with security too.

I'm too busy rummaging through my scattered thoughts to realize where Janine is taking me until I'm ushered into the employee lounge with Beth rushing in after us. I groan, knowing I'm in for some of Bethany's pampering.

My poor bestie is going to worry about me for the next week. Janine all but shoves me onto the leather couch to assess me.

"I'm fine," I rush out as Bethany flings herself in my direction. Her blonde ringlets are in disarray, and her hands flutter over me like I'm breakable or some shit. "Beth, breathe!"

"ME?!" Bethany fucking screeches. "You're already swelling, Blue! You need ice!"

Shit, she's right. Is it sprained? It can't be broken, but it is worse than when I pushed Declan. I wouldn't be able to move it if it were sprained, right?

"I've got some," a masculine voice interrupts our panic. Felix's worry makes me stiffen. I can't break. Can't panic. Not in front of him. "Blue?" he murmurs, his strong frame replacing Bethany's lithe one.

Where's Janine?

"What the hell are you doing here, jackass?"

Ah, there she is. The security of knowing my hard ass friend will ensure my safety helps me relax back into the couch. My frown begins to fade. Sleepiness makes my vision turn fuzzy around the edges, but I can't *not* focus on Felix.

His blond scruff is trimmed to perfection with his messy, dirty blond hair to contrast. The lines between his brows worry me, because there's no reason he should look this upset right now. I don't think I can handle his kindness.

What does that say about me that I'd rather have his cruelty than his care?

Trick question because I have the answer.

I'm a whole lot jaded and tremendously fucking sad. I can't shake the exhausting loop of wondering *why* over and over again?

So yeah. Maybe now, after everything and all the hurts, I'd rather Felix call me a weak ass bitch than look at me the way he is now. The pain and longing in his eyes awaken the vulnerability I've stashed away in the recesses of my soul.

He's coaxing out lip wobbles one frown at a time.

Twenty-Two

JARED

Blue's lip quivers, but she fights the tears I know are trying their damnedest to escape.

Fucking Christ. My heart breaks a little more as it pounds away in my chest. I'm not prone to anxiety, but receiving the call from Felix an hour ago that Declan was wasted and needed a ride freaked me out.

As a rule, my friend hasn't drunk enough to not be able to walk since college. Same with Roman, although the eldest Ledger brother is more strict about his consumption.

Hearing that my greatest friend of all time was so hammered he was passed out at Blue's bar made me sick to my stomach. Guilt yanked at my gut the entire drive to the club.

I should have pushed him harder about telling Roman years ago.

I should have checked on him hours ago.

I...I...I...

The selfishness of my thoughts made me shut down and focus on what I needed to do. I parked my car down the busy street and ran for the doors. There was something urging me faster and faster as I shimmied through the sweaty dancers. Once I saw the hulking man stiffen beside Declan, I knew I had to act fast.

D was in no condition to defend himself against an angry man almost double his size. *I won't be telling him that, though.* I didn't hesitate to yank Declan away, yet I soon came to realize it wasn't him the asshole was mad at.

Unfortunately, the crowd we got sucked into kept me from figuring out who the hulk was cussing out. Declan was spouting gibberish as the music blared around us. I didn't hold him back from trying to get back to the bar, thinking he'd left his wallet there or something.

I didn't realize until Felix came barreling through the sea of dancers that something horrible truly was happening. My attention was on keeping Declan upright and getting him home as soon as fucking possible.

Then....motherfucking *then*...

Felix staked a claim.

"GET YOUR HANDS OFF MY WOMAN!" he bellowed. Then began an aggression led by fear that I had never seen come out of Felix in our entire friendship.

My woman he said. It clicked in that moment because there's only one woman he would claim so viciously and blatantly.

Blue.

When the people parted and Felix bolted in a different direction, there was no choice. I had to follow. I clung to Declan's forearm and dragged him to the back room.

When we stumbled out of the crowd and into the shockingly glorious lounge area, I shoved Declan into a chair and ran toward the group surrounding Blue. Slightly out of her peripheral vision, I watch on as she blinks up at Felix.

My heart has yet to settle, and my nerves are firing every which way. The worrying only gets worse by the second as Blue so clearly fights another show of emotion.

"Please just leave me alone," she begs Felix, looking completely worn out.

Are we the reason? Beside me now, Declan sucks in a sharp breath.

Felix shakes his head and tenderly grabs her arm. "I can't do that, sweetheart."

She flinches at the first contact of ice. "Why not?" The distrust in her gaze makes me anxious.

"Well, A," Felix mutters, poking at her bruised skin. "Janine and Beth need to get back to the bar."

The woman who I believe is Janine scoffs. "Who are you to tell me what to do?"

Felix doesn't even spare her a glance. "I'm your boss. Just replaced your previous bar manager a few hours ago." With that, he levels Janine with a blank stare, waiting for her to argue. She doesn't and neither does Blue which freaks me out.

When he told us about accepting the position above her, Roman, Declan, and I thought it would be a disaster. I'm not seeing a tsunami of rage like I expected, though.

All I witness is the emotion in Blue's sparkling gaze disintegrating behind a shield of neutrality. *Come back, Bee.*

Cursing, Janine apologizes to Blue before rushing back out to serve drinks. I'm assuming with all three bartenders running back here, someone else had to step in for them. What do I know, though?

When the door slams shut behind the two women, Blue snaps, "So you're only here to fix an employee's hand, huh? Well, don't bother. Just give me a minute and I'll be right out."

Felix continues twisting her arm around, ignoring her quip. There's no way in hell she will be going back out there tonight. I don't need to ask Felix for his thoughts either.

"Just stop, Felix!" Blue snaps, trying to yank her wrist away from his gentle touch. She barely moves, and Felix catches her elbow before she can hurt herself.

"Don't move, Bennett." Felix grabs her jaw in a strong grip, making her eyes widen and my lungs stop working. "I swear to fuck if you hurt yourself..." he threatens more so to himself. Releasing Blue, he resumes icing her ache.

"Why do you care?" She no longer sounds mad, but there's a thick layer of uncertainty in her tone. The guilt that has lived inside of me for eleven fucking years expands and quivers in my soul.

Felix leans back ever so slightly and returns his touch to her jaw. "I've never stopped caring, sweetheart."

Defiance flashes in her gaze. She's closing herself off right in front of me. "Yes. You did. Nobody does what you did if they actually *cared*, Felix."

"Bee..." I murmur, needing her to see me. I need Blue to see me so maybe she'll realize how much I regret my childish choices. I *need* her to see me so maybe she will allow me to see her.

While the concept of her opening up to us sounds like a win, it sure as fuck doesn't feel like one.

My heart doesn't crack, it *shatters* when she sees me and Declan close by. Blue releases a scratchy sob that makes her entire body jolt. Her hands, one swollen, the other trembling, fly up to cover her face as she doubles over her lap.

Every atom of my body is tuned into every cry and shake of Blue's body.

While I *know* without a doubt that the woman before me is the strongest one I have ever met, I'm not naïve enough to think the strongest people are exempt from overwhelming turmoil.

My strong, beautiful, *vibrant* Blue is crumbling. While I'm heartbroken at the sight of her salty tears ruining her makeup, I can't help but feel relieved.

I've known since the moment we were reunited that the core of Erica Bennett has not changed. Blue is the persona she adopted to survive. To protect the energetic, happy girl who struggled to live on during her childhood.

"Blue, ca-can I?" Felix stumbles over his words which hurts me in a new way. He's always so damn sure of himself, I can't control the rise of my anxiety as I watch him reach for our woman with hesitancy that doesn't look right on him.

She only cries harder, swaying forward with her hands still covering her face, but she doesn't stop him.

This feels like a first step. *Please let this be our first step.*

Twenty-Three
BLUE

For as long as I can remember I've been fighting to shield the most innocent parts of myself. When my parents died, I began collecting bricks when other kids were collecting cool rocks.

They weren't tangible, but they were necessary. One by one, I stacked them around my heart in an attempt to block some of life's punches.

At six, my mom and dad died in a car accident. My aunt was my only living relative and took me in under the idea that she would get a lot of money for her *charity*.

My memory back then is fuzzy, so even if she did get money, it most definitely wasn't a fortune for becoming a guardian of an orphan.

Orphan.

I've heard that word many times in my life, often from other kids at school. I was the girl from the wrong side of the tracks. My nice jeans and pretty sweaters disappeared pretty quickly after I moved in with Aunt Linda.

God, I remember asking her where my stuff was. She pointed to a closet where I found dirty, ripped clothes that never kept me warm.

I made it through. At the age of six, I didn't know much beyond how much I missed my parents. Consumed by confusion, I just kept moving through school and getting my chores done. At that time I didn't much care about Linda's string of boyfriends.

I was uncomfortable, sure, but my parents' death led my emotions for a long time.

Until decent neighbors asked me to mow their lawn or shovel their driveways for some cash. As a preteen who was starting to realize how differently I dressed than other people, I jumped at the opportunity to buy myself new things.

I learned very quickly that I had to hide my nice stuff. Aunt Linda was a money-hungry bitch.

Still is.

Slowly but surely, I changed my image and my attitude. The pain of losing my two favorite people faded to a dull ache in my chest, but I blocked it out with a few bricks here and there.

Those bricks were the changes I made myself. My clothes, styling my hair, talking to new people, excelling in classes. I rewrote myself one piece of armor at a time.

Everyone forgot I was an orphan with a drug addict guardian who rarely fed me. I worked for every fucking ounce of happiness I had. The guys were drawn to the bubbly girl I had built myself up to be. It didn't take long for them to peek behind the wall I was steadily building around my sadness.

After many lighthearted conversations in the hallway, then meeting Roman and Felix, I allowed the gaps in my armor to shine with the endless pool of tears I had been drowning in since I was six years old.

Now? A moment of physical pain weakens that brick wall I've perfected. Over the years I've learned whom and how to trust. Declan, Roman, Felix, and Jared were on the strict *no trespassing* list right up until they showed me one singular fucking moment of care.

Just one.

A gentle touch, kind words, and worried eyes are my undoing.

One by one, bricks fall and break into pieces. One layer of mascara, a swipe of eyeliner, and a stroke of red lipstick at a time...Blue reveals her meaning.

Blue is the color of a bruise after a day or two.

Blue means sadness.

Blue relates to detachment and distance.

On a soul-deep level, I am all of those things. I am bruised. Sad. I am detached.

Everything I don't want to be but am, comes rushing to the surface in a wave that bellows *save me*.

Someone please save me because, goddamn it, I *hurt*.

Twenty~Four

DECLAN

There's nothing like the terrifying moment of a very large man hurting my girl to sober me right up. Fighting against the effects of alcohol was absolutely fucking awful.

I hated myself for tripping over my feet and swaying just enough to be shoved back. My God, I could have saved Blue from that asshole if I hadn't drunk so much.

Half stumbling with Jared to the back room where Felix disappeared into sucked too. The world kept tilting and turning. No matter how much I wanted to function properly, my body was hammered.

My mind felt sluggish too as I tried to comprehend the employee lounge. Confused and a little lost, I try to catch up with Felix and Blue's conversation.

Then Blue burst into tears at the sight of Jared. Every single instinct to help her and protect her fires on, burning the toxins from my mind.

Felix is there first. As much as I feel the gut-curling

need to scoop her onto my lap, I'm too far away. The man I love gets her instead.

Jared and I both step forward when Blue all but folds herself in half, but we stop when Felix stands and shuffles her around on the couch. My heart clenches at the sight of Blue curled into Felix's side with her head on his chest. Toned legs are thrown over his right leg, and white Vans are tucked under his left.

Unable to hold myself back from the heartbreaking display, I sit on the floor in front of them. I watch every tear soak Felix's shirt and study the lines on his face while he squeezes his eyes shut in pain.

The heaviness of her chest cracking sobs combined with the alcohol in my system gives me a headache. It's one I don't feel sorry about, though. Watching Blue cry her pain out is exactly what I deserve, and more.

I've left her alone in every vulnerable moment she's ever had for the past eleven years. All of this anguish could have been avoided had we listened to ourselves and not our parents.

Felix's eyes flutter open and find mine with perfect precision. My heart pounds for a whole new reason now. Red-rimmed, the look he gives me increases the visceral need I feel to join their cuddle.

There are no words, but I don't need any to know everything has changed. The way he's staring into my soul has never happened before. It's like he's *seeing* me for the first time.

Shuffling in the room goes unnoticed by me as I split my focus between Felix's heavy gaze and Blue. Her tears have slowed in the past few minutes. Aside from the occasional shudder, her breaths deepen.

A dull thunk beside me makes me jump.

"Is she asleep?" Jared whispers, rummaging through the small backpack he tossed down next to me. He produces a familiar steel water bottle.

"Yeah," Felix replies gently while continuing to tickle her arm.

Jared nods and tucks the water bottle back inside. "See if you can't scoop her up without waking her. Let's go home."

Felix does as our friend suggests, but I'm incredibly confused about how we got *here*. "What? We're taking her to *our* home?"

"I talked to Bethany, who said she'll come by to get Blue after her shift," Jared explains as if that's all I should know.

"Okay, but Blue's not going to like this. Like at *all*." How is it I'm the inebriated one, yet I'm the only one thinking logically? "She's going to be pissed when she wakes up in our beds."

"Then we'll give her Roman's." Felix has Blue in his arms, bridal style, as he says that. I blink, not knowing how to combat that, because it doesn't solve the problem of upsetting Blue. But also, do I really want to fight them on this?

I would fucking *love* to have Blue in our home. In our beds too, of course. So, yeah, I won't fight them on this.

With my mouth shut, I hold open the exit door in

the employee lounge Jared points us to. Blue's coming home with us. What'll it take to keep her there forever?

I'm not sure what Jared and Felix thought would happen when we basically stole Blue from her place of work, but I'm not surprised by the new turn of events.

"Where the *fuck* are we?!"

I whip around, my heart immediately stopping when Blue breaks the silence in the car. *Christ!*

Thankfully, Jared had already put our SUV in park before Blue woke up spitting mad. Jared and I jump, but our startled responses have nothing on the swift kick Blue lands on Felix's crotch.

"Fuck!" Felix shouts as Blue scrambles away from him. That's what he gets for hogging our sleepy girl. Honestly, I'm shocked she slept the entire seven minutes to our townhome.

She ignores the groans of pain and Jared's attempts to calm her down. Instead, she yanks on the child-locked door handle while cursing us out.

"Blue..." I try, but she doesn't listen, just continues to panic.

"Seriously! Let me out! *Please.*"

The distress in her plea has me unlocking the doors without a second thought. I follow her as she scrambles into the parking lot. Sucking in deep breaths, Blue puts her hands on her hips and tips her face to the night sky.

"Jeez..." she mutters to herself.

I'm debating whether I should keep my presence quiet or be loud so I don't scare her, but she turns around and glares at me. Jared comes up beside me and stiffens when he sees the exhausted, *angry* look on her face. Felix limps over to us as well.

Blue huffs and points a finger at us with one hand on her hip. "Don't *ever* do that again."

My mouth pops open, but before words can form, I choke when my brother ambles over from the backyard. "What did these idiots do exactly?"

"Jesus, why are you awake?" Jared wonders out loud.

Roman levels him with a bored stare. "You bolted out of the house like the world was ending, then none of you answered your phones. I waited up, hoping you were *alive*, jackass."

Jared, at least, looks like he feels bad. "Felix messaged me saying—"

"Nobody cares!" Blue basically fucking screeches, cutting him off. "Why am I here?! Take me back to work *right now*."

"There's no way in hell I'm letting you finish your shift, sweetheart, so get comfortable until Beth gets home." Felix must have lost a few brain cells when he got dick kicked. There's no way in hell that's going to calm her down.

"Excuse you?" Blue sneers and winces slightly when she slams her hands back on her hips. "You're not the boss of me."

Felix snorts, making dread pool in my gut. "Actually,

baby, I am."

"Don't call me baby," she snaps.

"Stop acting like one."

"Alright!" I clap, ignoring the sharp pain it causes in my skull. "How about we head inside before we wake the neighbors, huh?"

Blue doesn't hesitate. "No."

"Bethany will be home in an hour, Bee. Please, just come inside," Jared begs, sounding desperate.

Then Roman adds, "We have chocolate-covered almonds and that wine you like."

We've got her now.

Twenty-Five

BLUE

*S**hit.***

Some things never change. One of those being my obsession with chocolate-covered almonds. They're my kryptonite, and Roman just lit the fuse.

I'm pretty sure they're holding their breaths waiting for my answer, so I stay quiet for a few extra seconds in hopes they choke. Clearly, the offer of my favorite treat isn't able to quell the anger at the position they put me in.

Honestly, who puts a female in the backseat of a car with three men in the middle of the night *with the child-locks on?!*

They're so fucking lucky claustrophobia is the only thing I was battling in those long moments. I could have severe PTSD from being kidnapped or some shit.

"Lead the way," I finally relent. "But don't think I've forgotten about you taking me against my will and locking me in your car."

"You did what?" Roman growls. He grabs his younger brother by the back of his shirt and forces Declan to stay behind with him while Jared and Felix guide me to their townhome.

Hushed arguing follows me to their patio door. Now I'm the one holding my breath as I enter their space for the first time. There was a time when I knew their homes like the back of my hand. Now I have no idea how they like to live. Will their house be sterile like their parents'? Maybe they'll have fake fruit in their bowls.

The smell of perfume doesn't assault my senses when I finally inhale. It smells like a home. Like *my* home before my parents died. Sugar, bananas, cinnamon. A few steps later and I'm in their kitchen, where a loaf of banana bread rests on the stove. I can't stop myself from getting closer to the source of the glorious aroma.

"Roman bakes one every few days. Says it's because the smell reminds him of something," Jared says, opening a cabinet and pulling a few wine glasses down. "Little does he know, we all know how your mom did the same thing when you were young."

Tears prick my eyes, and I let him see the emotion when he hands me a glass of wine. *God, I miss my mom.* My memories of her are few, but I remember how absolutely loved I felt by my mom and dad.

I was fed great meals, dressed in nice things, hugged frequently, and asked about my day. Then they were ripped away from me, and all the warmth of the family I had cooled into greedy indifference.

Declan and Roman enter the kitchen behind me, Felix, and Jared, stealing all the oxygen from the room.

It's too much.

"Excuse me," I murmur, ducking between the brothers. With my wine glass cradled to my chest, I hurry back out the patio door and beeline for the cozy-looking couch.

I tilt my head back and count the stars to calm my anxiety. My nose takes in the fresh air, clearing it of yummy bread and the guys' fresh scent that cleared the cobwebs from my mind as soon as I woke up.

That's what was really startling. The way their cologne and aftershave scents combined into something that relaxed me into a deep sleep. Exhaustion stole my consciousness after crying my heart out, and I'm not surprised.

Sleep and I have a tough relationship. I haven't slept well in eleven years after I truly learned just how alone I was. Nightmares are occasional, but there's a constant stare down I have with my locked bedroom door every night.

Aunt Linda's boyfriends were all the same in their perusal of me. Some worse than others. But each night I swore my doorknob would rattle. I haven't been able to shake that lingering fear of what could happen if someone were to sneak in while I'm asleep.

So the fact that I slept through the guys moving me and driving us here is horrifying. If anyone can shatter the walls around my heart, mind, and soul, it's them. I've always known it.

Which is why it's incredibly inconvenient for them

to have moved to Chicago. Now Felix is my boss, and Declan owns the café in my building. *What the actual fuck?*

"Hey," a throaty voice interrupts my thoughts. Roman comes into view, extending a bowl of chocolate-covered almonds like a peace offering. "You forgot the whole reason you agreed to come inside."

I accept it and shift over so he can sit with me. He looks surprised, and I kind of am too.

"I'm tired," I say, explaining away my sudden acceptance of his presence.

The soft twinkly lights along the patio highlight his strong facial features. "I know," is all he says.

I study him as I feel bits of my wall crumbling. Roman, from what I have seen, has changed the most of the four of them. He used to be energetic and incredibly motivated. Always working and planning his future, Roman felt bigger than our high school life.

Remembering how determined and loud he was about his hopes and dreams makes me wonder what changed. He seems so quiet and reserved now. So different from the boy who felt worlds away from me.

Where I was focused on living in the present, Roman was future-oriented. I loved him, goodness I did. He was encouraging and smart. Teenage Roman made me *want* to live a life beyond the tragedies of my childhood.

Then he became one of them.

I start feeling curious after a few sips of wine combined with his gentle, if not sad, presence. Is it a bad idea to ask important questions that I don't know if I want the answers to?

"Why banana bread?"

His following response shocks me. "Would you like to hear a story, Blue?"

"Sure." I'm uncertain as fuck, but why not? My night, actually my entire day, has gone awry in some awful ways, so why not add to the emotional turmoil?

Roman takes a deep breath and leans his head back against the cushions. "There was this girl..."

Twenty-Six

ROMAN

The anxiety right now is horrendous. I feel like this is my only chance to grab hold of Blue and never let her go.

She opened the door to let me in when she asked about my baking habits. Blue knows the answer, so my interpretation is she's ready to hear me out.

So, I'll tell her our story.

"There was this girl. She was younger than me, but I was so envious of the way she swooped my brother under her wing. She was bright and so much fun. All I wanted was to be a part of her day."

I refuse to look at Blue while I get this out. It sounds so cheesy, but I feel like this is the only way she'll actually listen to me. Her silence encourages me.

"She only became more intriguing after I met her. My brother was infatuated from the beginning, and I thought *she'd be cool to hang out with*. But damn," I huff out a laugh. "She was so sweet and kind too."

I feel Blue's eyes move away from me. Ignoring whatever upset her, I continue because she *has* to know.

"Even my best friend, who didn't go to our school, was half in love with her within a month." No, I don't feel bad for telling Blue that Felix had feelings for her too. We're all flying by the seat of our fucking pants trying to ensure she forgives us.

"Rome—"

I cut her off because I'm on a roll now. "We spent all of our time together until I was nearing the end of senior year. College and the pressure of what my parents wanted me to do took my attention from my friends. I was more upset with the fact that I didn't hang out with my crush anymore, but I thought I was just doing what I was supposed to."

All of this is true. "I was a coward."

Blue sucks in a breath, hearing that my story is about to take a turn. I can't hide the pain in my voice as I recall the long string of bad decisions I made. Thankfully, she doesn't interrupt.

"My parents," I growl, "got in my head. *Our* heads. They loved to tell me and Declan that we were meant to go far in the world. And even if we brought you with us, your family would eventually catch up. They would ask us over and over again if a high school friend was worth risking our futures for."

I'm aware that I haven't apologized yet. Blue should know exactly what I'm apologizing for first. She's still listening, so I keep going.

"Felix's parents were friends with D's and mine, so of course they were saying the same shit to him. Sometimes I feel like it was easier for him to separate from the girl because he wasn't with her nearly as often. Though I still saw the pain in his eyes. Broke my heart."

"Jared, poor kid, had gotten so close to me, my brother, and Felix. His parents are saints and were immensely disappointed in him for cutting the girl out. He was young and did what his friends said was best."

A slight sniffle beside me tests my resolve. I take a deep breath and move on to the worst part of the story. "We decided that when she moved, it would be the best time to just completely cut ties. The most childish and cruel thing I've ever done was ghost the girl who brought life into our group."

I'm going to cry.

"Um," I clear my throat and close my eyes. "There was a lot of fighting and arguing. Leaving for college was the easy way out, and I took it. Felix moved in, which sounded great, but we spiraled together. We drank a lot, but not once did it drown our guilt. Christ, we were so fucking sad we almost failed our classes the first year. Had to get our shit together and work hard to get back on track."

"Grades were so important to you," Blue gasps out like that's the worst fucking thing I've said. It makes me angry that *that's* what she's commenting on.

"Not as important as *her*. I hate myself every day for what I did. More so after what happened to Declan."

"What happened to Declan?" She sounds scared and a little accusatory. I don't blame her.

I sigh, the self-hatred gripping my throat a little tighter. "He moved in with us when he graduated high school and enjoyed our lifestyle a little too much. Drank too much at a frat party then jumped off the roof and into a pool because it sounded fun."

Blue gasps and grabs my forearm, her touch burning me with passion and worry. "Holy shit! But he's okay, obviously."

I nod. "He wasn't for a bit. A few cracked ribs and some bad bruising. Concussion too. Mom and Dad were pissed."

"I'm surprised they showed up," Blue comments bitterly.

"Honestly, I'm glad they did. That was a turning point for all four of us. Mom and Dad called me a fuck up, then compared me to you and your family. They said horrible things about you and your aunt. Didn't even sugarcoat it with normal parental concern like they had done in the past."

"What did they say?"

I shake my head because if I tell her, then she'll stop touching me. "I'd rather not say."

Her nails dig in a little, making my focus flash to her determined face. "Please, Rome."

I study her, loving how her blue hair accentuates her eyes. Fuck, I can't deny her anything. "They said I was trailer trash like you. Like your family."

Blue snorts. "I bet they did. Believe me, you are far from trailer trash."

"That's not what upset me, Petal. Jared, Felix, Declan, and I cut my parents and Felix's parents off that day. We narrowed ourselves out, Jared moved in, and we continuously debated whether or not we should reach out to the girl we hurt."

She retracts her hand and crosses her arms. "But you didn't."

"No, we didn't. What a horrible fucking idea that was too. We thought we had done enough damage and that there was no way you'd forgive us. Christ, we didn't know if you had the same number or not."

"You fucking assholes didn't even *try* to figure out if I had the same number. News flash, I do, and I never blocked you. I should have, but it turned out I didn't even need to because nobody cared to contact me!"

"Blue," I whisper and feel relief when she doesn't stop me. "We cared. We cared *so much* it hurt. We were kids reeling from our string of bad choices. Honestly, we didn't have much to offer. I was fucking depressed, Felix barely controlled his party ways, Declan and Jared were totally aimless for a while."

"And what about me?!"

"That's what we want to know." Felix makes himself known. I knew they had been outside for a while now, and I'm glad they gave us the space to talk. "What happened after you moved, sweetheart?"

Blue jumps up, rage pouring off of her in waves. Headlights shine through the trees, drawing her attention and simultaneously making her deflate. Taking the four of us in, she zeros in on her backpack in Jared's hands.

He offers it to her with a nod and a sad look. "Bethany texted me, saying that's her, and you can head over to her place if you want."

Something that looks a little like jealousy flashes in her gaze when Jared mentions Bethany texting him. Hope flares that maybe there's still something between all of us. Some kind of connection we can play off of.

"Maybe next time," she says quietly, responding to Felix. Turning, she sniffs and begins her trek to the neighbors.

"Oh, and Blue!" I jump up, shouting for her. "The banana bread and the flower tattoos on my neck are a reminder of that girl we still love."

It's a bold statement, but I don't regret saying it. Not even when I hear her choke softly on a sob, because that means what I have to say affects her.

Blue doesn't look back, but she does say, "Good night."

Just that simple acknowledgment that the past ten minutes weren't a figment of my imagination makes me feel lighter than I have in eleven years.

Twenty-Seven

BLUE

"**K**nock, knock!" Bethany sings before cracking the guest room door open. The distinct coffee aroma she brings with her makes up for the morning sunlight she unleashes on my red-rimmed eyeballs.

"Thanks," I croak, taking the mug from her when she gets close. "You didn't have to."

Beth hums and sits on the edge of the bed. "I know. I wanted to, though." Her blonde ringlets are in two low pigtails, and she's makeup free. In a pair of sweatpants and a crop tank top, my friend looks stunning.

"What time is it?" I've refused to look at my phone all night. It's on do-not-disturb, but I have Violet saved as an emergency contact to bypass the silent mode in case she needs me.

"Seven-thirty," Bethany responds. She's watching me with a certain amount of hesitation that I'm not used to seeing. I've been pretty solid and reliable since we became friends. Now I'm a mess.

"You can ask," I encourage her. Knowing Bethany, she would wait forever before saying what's on her mind. She's the timid one in our group, for reasons that hurt my heart.

Blowing out a breath, she grabs my injured hand and gently cradles it in her lap. "Are you okay?"

I want to lie to her so fucking bad, but I can't bring myself to do it. "Not really."

"You're not crying."

Her observation makes me laugh. "I've been crying all night, babe. I'm fresh out of tears."

"Do you want to talk about it? What happened last night?"

Now that I've given her permission to ask about my shit, she's firing them left and right.

My knee-jerk reaction is to say I don't want to talk about it, but I really fucking should. After hearing Roman's point of view and what happened back then, I feel disorganized in my beliefs and feelings.

Instead of brushing her off, I pull my hand from her lap and take a couple of sips of my coffee. I'm going to need all the boost I can get to process this shit.

"First," I glare at her, "we're going to talk about you just sending them on their way with my sleeping body."

"Psh!" she huffs and waves me away. "They were so freaking worried about you, and I knew I'd be home soon to take over babysitting duty."

"I don't need to be babysat."

She eyes my bruised wrist. "Whatever you say. Now tell me what happened."

I relay everything Roman said to me last night. Her

face barely changes as she soaks it all in, making me wonder what's going on inside her head.

"Am I stupid for giving them any attention?" I blurt out at the end. Losing hours of sleep last night because of them feels crazy to me. I've lost a lot of time in my life thinking about the four of them, and I vowed never to allow it again.

Except that was before they became a part of every inch of my life again. That's dramatic, but that's how it feels. I'm being suffocated by memories and guilty looks on faces that are way too handsome to be human.

Of course, I'm losing sleep. Who wouldn't?

"I don't think that's the question you should be asking yourself, Blue," Bethany whispers, looking thoughtful. "I think asking yourself *why* you are giving them your attention is more important."

"That's easy. Because I deserve to know why they left me, don't I?"

She studies me. "But how will that serve you? What do you gain from this?"

My response is immediate. "Closure." As much as I've buried them, the past has a way of showing up.

Bethany frowns and hesitates. I nudge her, releasing her thoughts. "This seems like an opening, though. You've opened the door for them, now what?"

"Now I—" Shit. She's right. Now what? What the hell even is closure? "I say goodbye."

"That's great except it sounded like a question, Blue. Do you want to say goodbye?"

Damn her and her emotional intelligence. I open my mouth and close it a few times. "Fuck," I curse myself. "I should have already said *yes* if I knew what I wanted, huh?"

Bethany smiles sadly with a touch of slyness. "Yeah, hun. It sounds like you'll need to keep that door open for a while if you want to figure out if you should close it for good."

"What if I just slam it in their faces and forget about them?" I'm being pouty because this sounds like a fuckton of vulnerability that I don't want to share with four people who broke my heart.

"Then you wouldn't be much better than them..." she whispers, her eyes pleading with me not to rip her head off for comparing us. "I know there's really no comparing the circumstances, but your heart and the guilt I know you're susceptible to wouldn't be very rational about all of this. You'd fixate on *what ifs* because of what happened to you."

What if I block them and ignore them and something bad happens? What if they're hurt trying to get ahold of me? What if my actions cause them harm? They could fight and blame each other, ruining their friendships because of me.

"Yeah," Bethany agrees, having caught on to the spiraling going on in my head. "You're much better than that, Blue. Your heart is pure, and your anxiety is fierce. Making rash decisions out of anger will only make you vulnerable in the end."

"Anxiety feeds off of vulnerability..." I mutter, shivering. "They make me feel weak though, Bethany. I can't deal with that."

"Actually, I think that's exactly what you should be feeling. Think about it. You rarely have panic attacks or allow your triggers to make you freeze. You told me you panicked being trapped in their car last night. That you hesitated when that guy grabbed you because Declan was there. Your actions show you have room for growth, Blue. It's okay to pay attention to your cues. Those guys are challenging you, showing you your weak spots...Maybe that's not such a bad thing."

"Easy for you to say," I grumble, finishing my cup of coffee. "You make a good point, though."

She smiles and takes my cup. "I always do," she sings as she skips out the bedroom door.

Roman, Declan, Felix, and Jared unarm me. Can I really handle feeling defenseless again?

Beth is right. Maybe relearning my triggers after all these years will help me be even stronger. Letting a few of those bricks fall when I'm around them can't hurt that much, right? I'll do it for the self-growth.

I need time, though.

Twenty~Eight

BLUE

After a few weeks of soul searching, I've decided some grovel encouragement couldn't hurt. There's been some light stalker tendencies from the guys lately, and I hate to say it, but it feels endearing.

Some part of me feels bad that I've been dodging them and only exchanging pleasantries when necessary, but I really needed time to think. Their flowers, discounted lattes, and packed meals for me at work have broken down some of the shaky walls around my heart.

I've spent all my free time when I'm not working studying for the security test next week and training with Levi. The girls and I have met up for a few brunches, but I've avoided my usual cycling classes. It's weird knowing my instructor is Jared's sister.

The front door slams.

Skipping into the kitchen with a furrowed brow, my

cousin prepares to lay into me. "Ma," Violet scolds, crossing her arms over her chest, "you've been avoiding me."

Drumming my fingers on our kitchen table, I tuck my legs beneath me. Hmm, have I? If I'm honest with myself, then yes, I have been avoiding V when she's around.

But also. "Violet, you've been on a road trip for a week and a half. Then you spent two nights with your friends. I haven't had much of a chance to avoid you." The apartment has been quiet with her off on another adventure, which usually makes me feel lonely, but I used that time to think.

She jabs a finger at my cup and stomps her foot. Ignoring my statement, she questions, "Whose number is on your coffee?!"

I could have hidden Declan's attempts to get my attention, but I knew I'd have to tell Violet about them at some point. Especially now that I've decided to pursue a friendship with them. I've chosen to attempt peace. Attempt being the key word because I'm not sure how well it's going to go.

We live in the same city, though. They're neighbors of one of my best friends. Declan owns my favorite coffee place, Felix is my boss, and Roman's stalking me. As for Jared...whenever he sees me, he likes to update me on his parents. Asking about his mom and dad once, opened the door for more communication. I'm not mad about it, actually. I loved his parents, and hearing that his dad, Derrick, got into an accident makes me sad.

"Declan, an old friend of mine, asked his employees to put his cell number on my cups whenever I go in." Goddamn it, my heart warms a little saying it out loud.

I've rolled my eyes every time I see his phone number because it's the same as his old one. All he needs to do is text me. Miranda, one of my favorite baristas, says Declan is trying to *woo* me the old-fashioned way.

I'm not sure what that really means considering I've never been *woo*ed before. Yet even when I roll my eyes at Declan's phone number, I smile too.

"Blue, there's more. I know it." She's upset. This isn't about wanting gossip about my life, though. V struggles with abandonment issues, and with how close we have always been, my not letting her in on this part of my life must be heightening her anxiety.

Raising her for more than a decade created a bond between us. One that toes the line between parent and kid, and best friends. Our roles in each other's lives are a mix of the two, but we make it work.

She's my kid. I'm her Mama. We shoot the shit on Mondays over coffee, and I scold her on weekends for not texting me to let me know she's safe. I love Violet with my whole fucking heart. I gave her my slivers of sunshine so she could grow.

I sigh, feeling guilty for keeping her on the outside when we've been family for eleven years. "Any chance I can get away with just sharing the gist?" She raises a brow, and I take a shuddering breath. "V, I really don't know how I feel about telling you *everything,* but I'll share as much as I am comfortable with, okay?"

Her eyes soften, and she takes a seat beside me at the table. Her long, wavy blonde hair is styled to perfection. I wonder if she did a hair tutorial video today.

"Okay," Violet agrees softly and takes my healing hand in hers. It's still a little yellow from that jackass at the club, but it's on the mend at least.

Shit. "Okay, so you know my parents died when I was six. You also already know I moved in with your mom and grew up in her care from then on. It wasn't great..."

Violet snorts an angry sound. "No shit. If it was anything like after I moved in..."

"I—" Gosh, I don't want to make her feel bad, but she's an adult now. "It was worse. I didn't have anyone looking out for me at home. I spent as much time as I could at school and with my friends."

"Those friends...are those the guys?" Violet guesses.

I nod because it's mostly true. "They were my best friends in high school. Roman and Declan moved from another county. Felix hung around Roman outside of school, and Jared had always been in classes with me." Now I'm smiling. "We were inseparable."

"Erica! What the hell, girl?!" Felix shouts, running full speed at me. A squeal bursts from my lips as he swoops me into a big hug, spinning us around. "Seriously, where have you been?"

Goodness, his senior year muscles are becoming a distraction for me. I bite my lip when he sets me down. "I saw you four days ago, Felix."

He frowns and ruffles my hair a little, reminding me I'm just a junior in his eyes. "That's too long, sweetheart. Why didn't you come this weekend?"

"You mean on your boys' camping trip where you probably reeked like dirt and ass? No thanks." More like Aunt Linda forced me to stay home and clean up after her recent bender.

"Brat!" he growls, and tosses me over his shoulder.

I push on his ass, beat his backside with my fists, all while laughing and trying to get away from my friend. "Put me down!"

"Mama?"

I startle, my soft smile slipping. "Sorry, what?" Violet gives me a sad smile and tells me I zoned out for a minute. "So, Felix and Roman were a grade ahead of me, Jared, and Declan. Declan and Roman are brothers."

Violet nods, soaking in the information.

"I introduced Declan to Jared because the three of us shared a class. They became best friends because they were like two crazy peas in a pod. Declan introduced me to Roman, and Roman introduced me to Felix. Jared was there too, of course, because we were all attached at the hip."

"Hi, I'm Erica," I greet, waving a little. My toes bounce me up and down, the only outward show of anxiety. I'm outgoing these days—I can't be nervous to meet new people.

"Hi, Erica," the boy rumbles, making goosebumps rise on my arms. "I'm Roman."

"Like the Roman Empire?" I tease. Jared snorts behind me, and I smile. "Can I call you Rome?"

Roman smirks and leans against his locker like all hot guys do. "Only if I can call you, Petal."

I feel my nose scrunch. "Why Petal?"

"Because you have a few in your hair," he says, reaching forward and pulling, I shit you not, a blue freaking flower petal from my hair.

"Oh my god," I groan. "This is so embarrassing." So much for not being nervous. "I hit my head on one of those stupid hanging flowerpots by the side entrance."

Jared and Declan laugh but don't seem all that surprised. I'm easily distracted, or incredibly focused, however you want to look at it.

"Shut up, I was running late." I huff and brush my hands through my ashy blonde waves.

Roman fingers the soft blue petal and melts my heart. "Petal suits you."

"You're doing it again..."

I cringe. "Sorry. Where was I?"

"Sorry. Where was I?"

I really want to tease Blue for zoning out when it's obvious she's daydreaming about those men, but I don't. This is hard for her to talk about, and making fun of her would not be helpful.

"You hung out with them. Two are brothers. One lived in a different county. What happened to make you all separate?" I know it's going to be bad, especially seeing how Ma has been acting the past month or two.

Mama Blue has been acting like her old self. Lost in her thoughts, trying to get through each day like it's a hardship, watching her surroundings more. She's behaving as if we still live with my bio mom.

Stressed, worried, anxious, avoidant...

I may have been gone for a bit on my trip, but even over the phone she was acting strange. *I shouldn't have left.*

"Honestly, V...It's a stupid ass reason I'm trying to

come to terms with." *Oh, this should be good.* "Roman told me what happened. Or at least some of it."

"And?" I'm literally buzzing, needing to know like yesterday.

Ma sighs, looking freaking exhausted. "Small backstory. Roman and Declan's parents are very wealthy. Same as Felix's parents. The four of them are the best of toxic friends."

"And I'm assuming even before I came to live with you and Linda, she was poor?"

"You assume correctly," Blue confirms. "So what I gathered, their parents—not Jared's because they were always wonderful—didn't like me or Linda. They started whispering in their ears saying I would drag them down. Plus, they were going to move away for college, so what was the point in keeping me around, right?"

What the hell?

She takes a sip of her latte, but the caffeine doesn't lift her slumped posture. "They started pulling away when I was in senior year. It was easier for Roman and Felix to cut me out because they were touring colleges and planning their lives. Jared and Declan though." Blue shakes her head. "They got short with me. Started leaving me out of plans."

"Assholes!" I shout, pissed they could do that to her.

"It gets worse," Ma cuts off my impending rampage. "Your mom moved us from Seattle to Tacoma during my senior year."

"Let me guess," I spit bitterly, "new boyfriend?" *Fucking Linda.*

"Yep. And it was the perfect opportunity for them to ghost me. I moved an hour away and thought they'd still make the effort to see me like they did with Felix. *Nope.* They didn't answer my calls or texts for months."

I gasp, unable to control my reaction. "What the hell?! You never heard from them again until they moved here to Chicago?!"

How is she so calm right now? Blue deserves everything good in this world! She has raised me since I moved in with her when I was seven years old. Ma is the best person I know. She deserves to be cherished and flaunted. Most of my videos online are with her, or me gushing over how amazing she is.

I don't think Blue knows she is my main content, but it doesn't matter. My followers *love* my Ma, and I have many.

She eyes me warily. "Not exactly...Declan told me to leave him alone and move on. Felix..."

"Felix what?" I demand, ready to kick some ass.

Studying me for a moment longer, Blue thinks through something, then she seems to come to a conclusion. "Linda's Tacoma boyfriend scared me. He got rough a few times, pushed me around. Tried to get into my room at night."

"WHAT?! How come you never told me about this?!"

I'm going to be sick. Tears spring to my eyes, and my chest feels heavy under the pressure of this new information. No wonder Blue always has a pained look in her eyes. You just have to look past her flawless makeup, amazing outfits, and outgoing personality to see how deeply she hurts.

I just can't believe I'm only finding out about this now. How selfish am I that I don't know about this?!

"Violet, stop. I can see the guilt trying to eat you alive over there. I didn't tell you about any of this for that exact reason." Ma's tone is hard and unwavering.

"Please continue," I plead, needing to know the rest.

Her lips twist, and I don't think she's going to tell me anything else, but she does. "I asked Felix for help once. He said he couldn't help and reminded me I knew how to throw a punch. That was it."

"And then?" There's more, I know it.

"Then I finished high school and planned on moving out when I turned eighteen. You came to live with us, I saw the look on Linda's face and swore I wouldn't let you grow up the same as I did. So I stayed. We moved to Minnesota when her Tacoma boyfriend ditched her. I got my bartending license. Dodged Linda's one-night stands, saved money, got a boyfriend—"

"Oh! I remember your boyfriend! Josh right? Why did you guys break up?" He was around a lot and was nice to me, unlike Linda's random hookups Blue tried to hide me from.

Blue snorts. "He was a tattoo artist and got wildly offended when I wouldn't let him tattoo me but had someone else give me one behind my ear. He lost his shit, so I ended it. Then Linda got into some trouble with one of her fuck buddies, and we moved to Chicago when I was twenty-one."

Then my bio mom dipped when I turned eighteen,

six months ago. Haven't seen her since. Blue got us out of that nasty house four months ago and moved us in here. We've been happy ever since.

"Then *they* showed up," Blue whispers. "Roman told me they didn't realize how manipulative their parents were being until a long while later. They want me to listen to them. Hear them out because they were kids back then."

In her silence, I wonder what she's thinking. Clearly, she's struggling with what to do. "And now what?"

"And now?" She sighs. "I'm confused. Confused because I can understand they were too young to think maturely before and after. Confused because they're *everywhere* and I'm too tired to fight the pull to them."

"But they left you to be hurt, Ma..."

"That they did..." she mutters.

The doorbell rings, and I cringe so fucking hard. "So, speaking of them being everywhere..."

"Violet," she grits out in a warning tone.

"Roman was in the lobby with flowers looking sad. I gave him our apartment number and told him to come up in twenty minutes."

"Why would you do that?"

Shit, she's mad. "Uh, I didn't think the story behind him and the others would be that deep. But I was obviously wrong..."

"Obviously!" she snaps. Blue stands and takes a deep breath. "I'm sorry. It's okay. I was planning on giving them a *small* chance of being friends again. That conversation just brought up a lot of emotion."

"I'm sorry," I mutter, feeling really bad for putting

her in this position right after unloading her trauma on me. These guys left her to fend for herself *and* a depressed eight-year-old girl. I don't like the sound of them. I shouldn't have invited Roman up to see Blue without knowing the story first.

"Hey, Violet." Ma tucks some of my hair behind my ear. "This isn't yours to carry, alright?"

I shake my head a little. "What they did wasn't right. They hurt you. *So* many people hurt you."

"That's true. But I grew into who I am now because of those experiences. And who am I?"

Smirking, I answer, "A badass."

"Yup!" She kisses my forehead. "So let me deal with this, okay?"

"Okay." I trust her with my life and hopefully now that I'm older she can put more focus on herself.

And maybe four men?

Thirty

FELIX

I'm going to snap. All night long I tried to approach Blue at the club. Her friends kept getting in the way and shaking their heads at me. I'm their boss, so I could have demanded I see Blue. I didn't because manipulating the situation and using my position to force it won't win me brownie points.

We agreed to give Blue some space for a while because it was clear she needed time to think. She hasn't completely blocked us out of her life, which has allowed us to begin mending what we broke. I'm just getting antsy with only feeding her dinner at work.

I want more.

On the other hand, I'm so fucking horny I'm losing my mind.

I haven't so much as looked at another woman since I almost got to second base with Blue almost two months ago. I've been far too anxious to see her and fix things, so my priorities are fucked.

My poor dick is being neglected and, to top it off,

Blue is always dressed is the most amazing outfits. She's toned, curvy, and my God, her hair is amazing.

Then there's Declan. I'm pissed off because there shouldn't be *anything*—zero vibes—between us. But ever since that morning the coffee shop, there's more.

It's a mindfuck. I have Roman eyeing me left and right with threatening glares. Jared pokes at me, telling me I should figure my shit out constantly, and the man who's exciting me is avoiding me.

Declan's had the great excuse of a busy café in the morning and early afternoons when I'm free. Our work schedules make it impossible for me to see him, especially when he does everything in his power to run away from me.

Now it's Monday, and I know for a fact he won't be going into work today. Why? Because I lied and said I had to go in and do inventory this morning.

He's shown his patterns by not being wherever I am, so I'm forcing the issue now. We *will* talk this out.

The house has been quiet this morning with Jared at the high school today and Roman off stalking Blue. Or as he likes to call it, hanging around her apartment building in hopes of seeing her.

Poor guy is struggling. We're all worried that our efforts aren't appreciated. She hasn't told us to fuck off in a while, though, so that's a win.

I've been sitting at the kitchen island for about half an hour when I decide I've had enough. It's almost ten in the morning, and my anxiety is through the fucking roof. Declan and I need to sort this out right fucking now.

Swallowing the last sip of my black coffee, I stand and beg my heart to calm down. *I am in control.* Right? That's why I'm taking advantage of my lie so we can have this chat on my terms.

If I've learned anything about Declan's approach with me, it's that he will avoid it at all costs. And hide it too, obviously, because I had no fucking idea. Does that make me the bad guy?

Picking up my pace, I round the corner to the back hallway where Declan and Jared's rooms are. D's door is closed, so he must be asleep. *Well, not for much longer.*

I grip the handle and shove it open, my angst getting the best of me as I barrel through the door. "We need to talk," I demand, but I end up gasping on my words.

A strangled noise erupts from Declan just as his rock hard cock releases ropes and ropes of cum. Our eyes lock, his wide but full of pleasure, and I'd bet my ass that mine look similar.

Holy shit. Holy. Fucking. Shit.

"Fuck, Felix," Declan groans, his voice thick with a remaining moan. His hips buck one last time, and saliva pools in my mouth. I swear my dick jumps with his movement too.

My chest vibrates as if something inside of me is shifting with all the new possibilities before me. It's been a long damn time since I've fucked around with a man. But Declan looks like something else.

D is all man who looks ready for round two.

"Felix, don't," he mutters, but he doesn't cover himself.

I'm really not sure what he's saying no to, so I step toward him. Thinner than me, Declan looks a bit more cut and firm. I lick my lips, wanting to taste the divot between his six-pack. Christ, I don't even know what I came in here to say to him. I never decided how I felt.

Right now, with him naked like a fucking offering, I'm not sure there is any other choice I would consider.

"Felix, stop. Please. Not like this."

I halt, realizing I'm just about at the foot of the bed. His words make me pause and reassess. The look on his face, while still full of lust, has a fuckton of wariness now.

"Shit," I curse, dragging my hand through my hair. I turn away. I hear the bed move and fabric being tossed around, but I don't look. Holy shit, I just watched my friend orgasm and was prepared to lick the cum right from his stomach.

What is wrong with me? I've just ruined everything.

A firm hand on my bicep stops me, and I close my eyes, not willing to make him uncomfortable again. "Felix, it's okay."

I can't help my laugh. "It definitely was *not* okay."

"Can you look at me, please?"

"No." Although that might be the better option since I keep seeing his hot fucking body behind my eyelids. *Fuck, he's burned into my brain.*

He pushes me, bothering me just enough for my eyes to snap open and glare at him. Declan's grin is small, but it's there. The relief I feel is immense.

"Calm down, man. It's not a big deal."

The fuck did he just say to me? "Excuse me?"

He rolls his eyes, and the image of spanking his ass appears before I can stop it. "We've seen each other naked before. It's fine."

Ah, I see what he's doing. Running from me and his feelings like normal. "Don't. Don't fucking do that, D. I came in here to talk about your crush on me."

He hums but fails to mask the hurt in his gaze. In a pair of boxers and a black sweatshirt, he looks cuddly. I shake that thought away, feeling less and less in control by the moment.

"Exactly, Felix," he says sadly with that damn grin still in place. "It's *my* crush. No reason to bring you down with something one-sided."

Fuck no. Absolutely not. I advance on him and take satisfaction when his eyes widen. Chest to chest, I still have a few inches on him, so I use it to crowd his body with mine.

"What exactly do you think I almost did a moment ago, Declan?"

He gulps. "I—I don't—"

"No. Stop bullshitting. Tell me what you think I was going to do after you moaned my fucking name." I'm angry. Not with him, but with myself. I'm so confused, yet my instincts aren't taking the hint to back off and reevaluate. All I know is I *need* Declan to admit he saw me salivating for him and *demand* I admit my own feelings too.

"You looked like you were going to eat me."

He gasps as I grip his jaw. "Good job," I mumble and hold him a little tighter so he knows who's in charge.

Control. "Now tell me why you asked me to stop when I know you want me too."

He gulps, and fuck me does it make my balls ache with the need to release. Preferably on or in him. "I didn't—I don't want *this*," he waves a hand in the minuscule space between us, "to only be about sex. I— Fuck, Felix. That's not all this is for me."

I narrow my eyes. "And who said it was only sexual for me?"

He snorts, the bastard. "I have nothing else to go on, asshole."

"Then let me talk," I snap.

He pushes me again. "You won't stop asking questions!"

"And you won't stop hiding from me!" I shake him a little, making our mouths brush ever so slightly. His breath hitches, and my lungs tighten. Or maybe that's my pants.

"What am I supposed to do?!" he retorts, and I'm ready to shout right back when a voice that absolutely *should not* be here interrupts.

"Next step would be kissing."

Blue.

Thirty-One

BLUE

When I opened my door to greet Roman half an hour ago, I was not planning on inviting him to the gym with me. But when he pouted about not being able to find a decent place to work out, I caved.

I definitely didn't think I'd be riding with him to their townhome so he could change and get a water. And I *abso-fucking-lutely* did not assume I'd find Declan and Felix looking like they are ready to fuck each other's brains out.

Jesus.

I'm woman enough to admit that the scene I'm witnessing is the sexiest thing I've ever seen. And yes, my panties are soaked. Their arguing makes this even hotter. When Declan asks what he's supposed to do, it's pretty fucking obvious.

"Next step would be kissing."

Amusement bubbles up my throat as Declan and Felix jump and dart their eyes toward me. They don't move apart, though, which is interesting. You'd think with something clearly so new, they'd be freaking out about being caught.

"Do you need help?" I ask. Their ragged breathing is the only response I realize I'm going to get.

Declan gulps and flashes his gaze to Felix who hasn't moved. *I think they actually do need help.* Kicking off the doorframe, I saunter over to them doing my best to keep my heart locked up tight.

The scent that encompasses the two of them as I get closer makes my arousal skyrocket. Sex and cologne. *Goddamn.*

Against my better judgment, I step into their space and wrap my hands around their necks. I must be drunk on the sexual tension in the room because I forget all about the *just friends* policy I made with myself.

My heart pounds and my clit throbs with each pulse too. I'm so focused on their parted lips, mine start to tingle. "Like this," I murmur and pull Felix down to me first.

He sucks in a breath right before our mouths collide. Taking control of our kiss is shockingly easy considering he's such a dominant guy. I nip at him and force my way between his lips. Chills race down my spine when our tongues touch, making me grip Felix's neck harder. He groans and begins to battle me for control, but I split when I feel myself slipping too far into the addictive energy that is Felix Morel.

Our three bodies are flush when I pull away from Felix. Quickly, I break eye contact with him because while I'm horny as hell, I can't form that connection with any of them. This is just about the sexual tension.

"Your turn," I whisper and yank Declan toward me next. His kiss is less surprised and slow to start, but it's also sweeter. For a man who's a bit ballsy and chaotic, his mouth is tender, and his tongue is gentle.

My tummy swoops and my heart flips, making me end the kiss sooner than the one with Felix. "Now, you guys," I croak and push them together. Just as their mouths meet, I slip away and rush quietly to the door.

Quickly closing the door behind me as softly as I can, I blow out a breath.

"Want to talk about it?"

"Ah!" I whisper shout, my hand going to my chest in fear. "Jesus, Roman. You scared the shit out of me."

He raises a brow and smiles a little. "Well?"

So he clearly saw all of that. "No," I grumble, rushing away from Declan's room like the hot hellhounds are nipping at my clit. *Wait, NO.* "Let's get out of here."

Roman laughs, but follows me through the kitchen and outside to his car. Thankfully, Levi's gym is only a few minutes from here so Roman can't demand answers from me.

Fuck, I just kissed Declan and Felix. Then they kissed each other! This was not the plan.

As soon as I get us through the front doors of the gym, I'm ready to bolt. "I'm going to the bathroom. See you in a minute," I mumble and rush away from Roman.

Unable to get the feel of their lips out of my mind, I curse myself for my hussy choices. Roman was calm as a fucking clam the entire drive here, all the while I was losing my shit. Silently, of course, because he doesn't need to know I'm in the middle of a horny crisis.

Slipping past a few women changing, I close myself in a stall. As much as I would love to bang my head on the door, I don't—that's gross.

I do my business and dab the built-in panties of my shorts. They're about as dry as they're going to get, and they're only going to get wetter if I have to watch Roman workout.

As I wash my hands and make my way back out to the main gym, I wonder if there's a way I can get out of this. I'm flustered which gives Roman an advantage. If he has the upper hand *while* lifting weights, my boundaries are toast.

Well, let's be honest, they incinerated the moment I saw Declan and Felix together. What a fucking choice that was.

I blink and suddenly I'm in the twilight zone. Roman and Levi waltz out of Levi's office grinning. *How long was I gone?*

Roman shakes my friend's hand. "This is great, man. Thank you for the opportunity. What time do you want me here tomorrow?"

"Does nine work? We'll go over some basics of the

gym and work out your schedule." Levi looks so excited I almost feel bad for bursting their bromance. *Almost.*

"What's going on?" I snap, crossing my arms as I stop in front of them. They make me feel puny, but I shake it off. "Did you seriously just hire the enemy?"

"Enemy?" Roman asks, looking hurt and surprised.

I wave him off. "Levi doesn't know I'm attempting to forgive and befriend you so this," I gesture between them, "is against girl code."

"How do you know Rome?" Levi asks me, looking confused and worried. *Good.*

"You mean Roman? One fourth of the asshole squad who ghosted me in senior year?" I can't help it; I stomp my foot like Violet did this morning. *Where's my water bottle?*

"Shit. Fuck! You're joking. Tell me you're joking!" Levi grabs my forearm, looking a little green. He glares over at Roman who I refuse to look at right now. "Rome?"

"Stop calling him that," I growl, pulling my arm free. That's *my* nickname for him. "You knew what he did, Levi. All's just forgiven because you need a position filled? You're my best friend."

Shit, the anger is fading behind the hurt in my tone. My eyes burn a little too. Today is a complete mess. I want to go home.

"Petal..." Roman murmurs. "I met Levi in college. We were gym buddies. I didn't know you were friends. I'm sorry."

Levi's jaw grinds as he studies his college friend.

"Son of a bitch, dude. This sucks. *You're* one of the guys who hurt my girl?"

Something shifts in Roman's eyes making me stand up taller and take notice. "*Your* girl?" Roman snaps, stepping forward threateningly.

My pussy flutters, enjoying the possessive reaction. I grab Roman's shirt and tug him toward me. "Levi's married. To Kevin."

"Oh." Rome deflates, almost curling around me in relief. Then he perks up. "Wait really? Congratulations, man!"

What the hell is happening?

"Thanks. We need to have a chat, though," Levi declares, glaring at Roman. "Blue, go do your warm-ups. We'll be there in a minute."

Not once does he take his eyes off of Roman. Slightly giddy over the fact that Levi's going to lay into Roman a bit, I skip over to my friend and kiss his cheek. Roman makes a sound of indignation, but I scurry away with a mischievous feeling buzzing in my spine.

If Rome can handle my buff bestie telling him off for his behavior, then we'll be another step closer to making amends.

Thirty-Two

T eaching high schoolers any form of math is exhausting. Even the prep work, for fuck's sake. They don't want to be there—except for the select few. The thing about math is that what I'm teaching now is not what these students' parents were taught. Therefore, these kids don't have much help at home.

Classes haven't started yet, but I guarantee I'll have a few people tell me I'm teaching them wrong. It's hard when there is one right answer but many ways to get there.

Something clearly happened between the time I left today and right now. I'm seeing the end result, but how the hell did we get here?

Blue's sitting on the island in the kitchen, arms flailing as she tells a story about someone handing Roman his ass at the gym today. She laughs, and Roman's face turns red, but he smiles good-naturedly.

Not only is Blue Bennett willingly hanging out in

our home, but Declan and Felix are pressed together on separate stools watching Blue with wonder in their eyes.

"What's going on, guys?" I ask hesitantly.

Blue's eyes widen when she sees me, but she doesn't move. Instead, she gives Declan and Felix a pointed look.

Felix sighs and turns to me. "We kissed."

Holy shit. My backpack clunks to the ground. "Who?" There are so many options.

"Declan and I," Felix answers, blushing slightly. I notice his hand on my best friend's thigh, and my mood brightens exponentially.

"Fuck yes!" I holler, ready to party. "About damn time."

"That's not all," Roman drawls, leaning against the fridge looking smug.

Blue huffs but otherwise doesn't say anything. I narrow my eyes, incredibly intrigued and shocked to see her in our home, but I'm too anxious to point it out. *Please don't leave.*

"Blue kissed Felix," Declan announces. "And me," he adds with a shit-eating grin.

I choke on fucking air. "Holy shit. What? Why? How did this happen?!"

"Maybe I should go..." Blue wiggles off the counter, but I jump in front of her. "Jared," she warns.

"No. Fuck, please don't go. Tell me about today. Why are you here? Not that I don't want you here but-but how?" Begging isn't a good look on me, I know that. But

I'm so lost and jealous and so fucking excited I'm breathing funny.

Blue nibbles on her bottom lip, which my dick notices and perks up. "I shouldn't have kissed them. The tension got the best of me, but hey now they're together, so you're all welcome."

That's a lot to unpack, but I urge her on. "What else?" *Please stay, please stay, please stay.*

"Apparently Rome knows another one of my friends. Levi hired him as a personal trainer then brought him back into the office and laid into him about your piss-poor decisions. Oh!" Blue smiles big and glances at a red-faced Roman. "Then Levi proceeded to out-bench Roman. All in all, it was a fine time. I'm feeling avenged."

"And now you're here?" I'm still not understanding what suddenly changed. She had been giving us the bare minimum for weeks after Roman poured his heart out to her.

"Mhmm," she hums.

I glance at the others who are eyeing Blue like she's going to bolt at any moment. I can practically feel them begging me not to push her away, but we can't dance around the subject without it coming back to bite us in the ass.

"What changed? Do-Do you forgive us?" I stutter over my words, the enormity of the situation strangling me for a second.

Her lips twist, a sign that she's anxious as well. Or at least that's what it used to mean. With her hair up in a high ponytail and her body in tight workout gear, she looks ready to fight, but her nervous behavior tells me otherwise.

She needs comfort and stability when she gets like this. Everything she never had growing up with her aunt. Everything we stole when we ghosted her.

"I've had time to think..." Blue mutters, twisting her hands in front of her. We all lean forward to hear her better. "I understand we were young and mistakes are made. Friendship while being near each other often seems like the mature path to take."

"So, you forgive us?" Declan sounds excited and way too hopeful. He's about to have his hopes shattered because the angry glint in Blue's eyes makes it obvious what she's thinking.

"Fuck no." She glowers at him. "I said I *understood*. You haven't done enough to mask the bad with good yet, Declan. There's so much hurt that I don't know if you'll ever make it better, but I'm willing to let you try. I'm willing to try..." Blue adds in a much softer tone, making my heart ache for her.

This can't be easy, but she's offering an olive branch. We'd be stupid not to take it. I reach out and trail my fingers down her bare arm. "Thank you, Bee. We'll make sure you won't regret it."

I watch with fascination as she releases a tense breath. "I hope not. But you need to understand I don't have a lot to give. There's a lot I *won't* give. I have Violet to think about, and I refuse to be broken ever again. Shallow friendships are all I'm willing to offer."

Right now, I add for her because there's no fucking

way we'll only be friendly. Hell, she kissed my two friends today.

"Alright," I agree without letting on that we're going to fight for more. "Still want to go?"

Blue glances at all of us one last time. "Yeah. I should get home. See you later," she blurts and basically runs out of our house.

Not a moment after the door slams closed, Declan says what I've been thinking. "We're all in agreement that her *friendship* thing is bullshit, right? I'm going to grovel for way fucking more than that. And you're coming with me," he says to Felix, dragging him on this new romantic adventure.

Felix smirks and nods. "'Course. She can't kiss us then say shit like that. As far as I'm concerned, she's ours."

"Yeah," Roman agrees softly looking toward where we last saw Blue.

I nod vehemently. "Fuck yeah. So how do we grovel hard enough not only to earn her forgiveness, but convince her to fall in love with us?"

Declan has the answer. "Don't give her space to think. We have to be there every damn moment we can, like we used to be. We can't let her demons get to her ever again."

Just as we used to do in high school. Only this time we won't fuck it up.

Thirty-Three

BLUE

"What's the verdict?" Janine eyes me over the rim of her mimosa. Her eyebrow is daring me to give her the wrong answer.

I don't know the answer. "I'm not sure. What do you guys want to do?"

"Blue, it's *your* birthday we're planning. Don't ask us what we want." Dakota looks appalled. "Violet, talk some sense into her."

Violet's head snaps up from her phone, and she immediately puts it face down on the table. *Weird*. "What did you say?"

I narrow my eyes. Does she have a boyfriend? Girlfriend maybe? She's been wrapped up in her phone a lot in the past few days. If she were younger, maybe I could get away with searching her phone for creeps, but we're past that point. *Sadly*.

"Blue asked us what *we* want to do to celebrate her birthday. I think that's crazy," Dakota explains not picking up on Violet's distractedness.

Rolling my eyes, I take a sip of my screwdriver and listen to them toss out ideas I might like. All the options sound just fine, except there's something missing from the plans. Or a few someones are missing from the guest list.

"It's a few weeks away still. Let's wait to plan it." My suggestion falls on deaf ears. It's only been a week since I kissed Felix and Declan. Work has been busy, and with Violet being home more recently, I've been too distracted to shoo the four men away.

If I thought they were everywhere before, I was mistaken.

Felix takes his breaks with me, where we normally just sit in silence and sneak peeks at one another. He's asked me about my interest in the security team position, which I don't mind talking about.

Declan makes my coffee every morning with a soft smile and encouraging words for the day ahead. He's become a bright spot in my mornings that I didn't see coming.

Roman still brings me flowers and even brought takeout up to our apartment on Thursday. To say Violet was excited about her orange chicken was an understatement. I'm sure I'll be seeing him at the gym more now that he's almost done with training too.

Jared texts me fun facts about math, updates me on his family, and asks invasive questions about my day because—well—he's Jared. We haven't breached the subject of my not going to cycling class, which I hope means his sister isn't gossiping about my attendance.

"What if we just figure out where we're going for now, then we can decide on times?" Bethany's attempt to compromise on the planning is appreciated.

"Rooftop drinks then Serpent's," I decide on a whim because A, they won't question it, and B, there's a high probability the guys will be at Serpent's Kiss anyway.

Or I could just invite them. But what would that mean?

The girls start discussing rooftop bars that have fire pits because there's a high probability that mid-September in Chicago will be cold. I start zoning out until Bethany stiffens and nudges me.

"Incoming," she whisper hisses.

I quickly take a big sip of my orange juice and vodka to prepare myself for whoever she sees. Janine glares over my head, and Dakota's frowning. Violet smiles and waves, confusing me.

"Where's my latte, barista boy?" my cousin pouts and crosses her arms.

Fucking hell. *Declan.*

"Sorry, squirt. Didn't think we'd be running into you ladies here."

I take another sip of my drink as the hairs on my arms tingle with awareness. I'll have to acknowledge them eventually, but if I could get a little buzz going that'd be great. Maybe I'll feel much better about being caught off guard then.

Who am I kidding? All they do is catch me off guard.

My chair shifts and creaks as it's pulled away from

the table. Fighting back the gasp that tries to fly from my mouth, I quickly set my glass down and look up. Felix smiles down at me, looking absolutely yummy in his black T-shirt and jeans.

"Good morning, sweetheart," he rumbles, and like the ballsy bastard he is, he swoops down and kisses my cheek.

The breath in my lungs explodes out of me in exasperation. "Hi," I breathe, sounding far more affected by his lips on my skin than I'd like to admit.

Felix just smirks and pushes my chair back in. Glancing around, I notice only Declan and Felix are here. I wonder if they're on a date.

"Good morning, Blue." Declan greets me with a kiss on the top of my head. I swear their only goal lately is to make me flustered. *Wait*—Violet's greeting finally registers. "Violet, you've been getting free drinks at the café?"

Violet smiles and nods. "Yep! Declan hooks me up with an extra shot of espresso too."

"Winning my woman over without gaining her friends and family's approval is just stupid," Declan explains like that's all the information I need. Then he swipes a grape off my plate, making me scowl up at him. *Damn it, why does he smell so good?*

Bethany leans forward, capturing my attention. "Wait, is that why Roman was making sure the storm didn't damage my garden and patio furniture the other morning?"

"Well, that and we *are* nice guys, contrary to popular

belief." Declan isn't holding back today apparently. Where's the server when I need another boost of vodka?

"And the snacks in the break room?" At least Janine sounds like she's scolding Felix, but the asshole just smiles and nods. My friend huffs but grumbles out a thank you.

"Oh!" Dakota puts her hand in the air. "I had a few teenagers come to the salon saying they were referred by their new math teacher, Mr. Jones. Jared?"

"Yeah, that's Jared. He had a stack of your business cards displayed at the high school meet and greet. Did he send them with a stack of nerdy math puzzles too?" Declan looks excited as he converses with my friends.

My heart can't take it. This is more than shallow friendships. I had no idea they were doing these things for my friends too. "Well, we are eating so—"

"No, but we had a package dropped off with a ton of puzzle workbook thingies. My clients are *loving* them," Dakota gushes, cutting off my dismissal.

Felix, who has no boundaries, studies Beth's notebook over her shoulder. "What are you guys planning?"

"Blue's birthday celebration. We're doing a rooftop bar then dancing at Serpent's Kiss," Beth says without thinking as she doodles another heart on the page.

Felix's head snaps up really fast, then his eyes land on mine. "September twenty-eighth, right?"

"Yup," Beth hums, still fucking doodling.

The way Felix is staring at me makes my spine tingle and the back of my neck heat. He looks so intense, like he's daring me to fight him for whatever reason. Bethany is the one I'm eager to fight right now.

Then Felix goes and invites himself to my birthday. "We'll be there." *Motherfucker!* "Come on, D."

Declan waves as Felix pulls him out of the restaurant by his belt buckle. Sons of fucking bitches.

Thirty~Four

DECLAN

The sense of loss when Blue pulls away is immense, but when Felix's mouth slams against mine, a whole new fire roars in my veins.

I once thought I could match Felix in dominance, except now that I'm finally kissing him after all these years? There's no way. Like a fucking savage, Felix grabs my jaw and wastes no time tongue fucking my mouth.

His enthusiasm could trick me into believing he's wanted me for years too. Knowing the truth doesn't make this moment any less powerful, though. The momentum of our connection brings our hips together, and it's all I can do to keep from blowing another damn load.

His dick grinds against mine, sending lightning up my spine. Felix bends me backwards enough to make my neck ache. I moan and reach for the back of his head to keep me steady, yet I don't feel small fingers in my way.

Swirling my tongue with Felix's, I relish in the sensation only to realize I'm missing one I started with. Blue's no longer forcing our makeout session.

"Whatcha thinking about?"

I blink, realizing I've been staring at the side of Felix's face for however long I was lost in that memory. "Was thinking about our first kiss with Blue." Admitting that doesn't feel weird.

In many ways, Felix is still one of my best friends. While we have crossed that boundary into *more than that*, we haven't done anything more than slip each other the occasional tongue in our quick kisses.

The sexual tension is off the fucking charts, but we've done our due diligence to not be alone very much this past week. I was serious when I told Felix I don't want *this* to just be about getting off.

I'm in love with him. I want more.

"I can't believe we didn't notice her escaping," Felix grumbles, still beating himself up over it.

I broke the kiss and shouted for Blue only to realize she had left and closed my bedroom door. We ran out of the room, hoping to find her, but she wasn't there. It wasn't until that afternoon, when Roman came home with Blue in tow, that we figured out what the hell she was doing at the house that morning in the first place.

As much as we wanted to pester her about the sexy as fuck kissing, she looked happy and prepared to stay. Blue is a flight risk it seems, which Jared proved not fifteen minutes later when he started asking her questions. It's as if she's comfortable being around us if we don't push.

So maybe if we're simply *around* her, then trust will build so she can finally open up to us. And yes, I know we can't force her to open up. *That's not how vulnerability works.* Roman schooled me pretty hard on that already. That doesn't mean I can't lay some serious groundwork in the form of free coffee and big smiles for her to let her guard down. Which, I will add, is proving to be harder than I thought.

"Dec?"

I figured Violet was putting in a good word for me since I've extended my groveling to her as well, but Blue looked surprised yesterday morning when she heard about how we've been looking out for her friends this past week.

"Declan."

I'm considering buying a notebook for all my groveling ideas. Jared's sister reads a lot of betrayal and grovel books, so I've been gathering some ideas. Honestly, what some of those MMCs have done to their women...*holy fucking shit*.

Reading the FMC's—I think that's the right term—point of view has been absolutely painful and totally enlightening. Maybe I'll download some audio versions and have them on around the house so the others can soak it all in too.

I can't imagine even a fraction of the pain we caused Blue, but reading fictional possibilities is giving me some heartbreaking perspective.

"Declan!"

Fear shoots through my ass, making me jump and shout. "Jesus, Felix! What the hell?!"

My new lover, partner, boyfriend, complicated *something* glances at me with bewilderment. *We haven't talked about it much.* I'd venture to say we're in the *exploring what this means* stage.

"I've tried to get your attention like a thousand times."

Willing my heart to chill the fuck out, I raise my eyebrows at him to lighten the mood. "Wow, are you okay? Since when are you dramatic?" Felix is a hardass, and yes, he does have a *hard ass*. He let me grab it on Wednesday.

"Are *you* okay? I've never seen you think so hard," he fires back, flicking his blinker.

"Har, har," I mock laugh and punch his hard thigh. *I wish it were his ass.* Spanking Felix is against the rules—I learned that also on Wednesday. I'm still waiting for the spanking he's been threatening me with.

He scowls and slaps my left pec. "No hitting the driver," he scolds in a throaty voice that makes my dick perk up. I flick his nipple just as he's throwing the car into park. "You're asking for a pounding." *More threats.*

"You won't spank me, Felix." *Just keep poking...Just keep poking...*

His eyes darken as he leans across the center console. "I said *pound*, Declan. Your ass is asking for a pounding."

Oh...*Ohhhh.* "Fu—" My moan is cut off as Felix grabs the front of my polo and absolutely devours my mouth.

He breaks the kiss way too fucking soon, like Blue

did, and twists my nipple a little when I try to chase him for another one. "No more. We have family to visit."

Shit, fuck. "They're going to be pissed." I cringe.

"Rightfully so," Felix responds in a grave tone.

Jared's parents demanded a family dinner after his sister spilled the Blue beans.

Told them what, I don't know. But we're about to find out.

Thirty-Five

BLUE

"Is there anything you want to talk about?" My nervous system is on high alert as I ask Violet that dreaded question.

For the love of everything good and holy, I hope she doesn't have anything gross to say to me. She may be my cousin by blood, but I became a parent to her when she was a sweet young girl. *Please don't tell me a sex story...*

She blinks away from the corner of the living room. She had been staring at it for the past few minutes. Maybe longer. I don't fucking know, but she's setting me on edge.

"What?" She frowns at me.

I tense a little in response to her blank look. "V, you've been acting a little strange lately. Everything okay?"

"Oh," she mumbles and blinks *again*. "Yeah. I think I'm gonna go to bed. I'm tired."

Before I can point out that it's not even seven P.M.,

she's shuffling down the hallway with her phone lighting her face. "What the hell..." I mutter, feeling conflicted. She's eighteen, but damn it, she's still that eight-year-old who used to cry in my arms when Linda fucked off to who knows where.

I'm sure every parent feels conflicted about how much is appropriate to pressure their kid. I just didn't think it would feel this *horrible*.

Am I doing enough? Have I not been as present as I should have been? Does she feel safe talking to me about stuff? Do I *want* to hear about some stuff?

Groaning, I flop back onto the couch and grab my water bottle. My fingers trace over the cool surface in search of dents. I'd hate to replace another one, but sometimes it's necessary when my comfort item moonlights as a weapon.

The TV flickers as the most recent dating show continues to play its toxicity, but I ignore it. I should be able to thrive in uncertainty, but I really fucking wish life could feel balanced for once.

I don't know what to do about Violet, and I definitely don't know how to move forward with Roman, Jared, Declan, and Felix. They're doing all the right things even if they are slightly annoying at times.

Each interaction reminds me not of the boys they used to be but of how much they've grown. And I don't mean physically, although *yes*. I mean emotionally, socially, and logically. They're adults in their late twenties/early thirties. I'm experiencing how they've learned from life's lessons.

The main one is how observant they are. I'm not

sure who realized giving me too much time to think was the wrong move, but it was smart. Left alone with my jaded issues wouldn't give me a good outlook.

Free coffee, food, kindness, communication, and company? Now those provide a great outlook on the future. *But what kind of future do I want with them?*

My phone buzzes on the coffee table. Once upon a time I would have been confused by random late-night text messages, but now there are many possibilities of who could be texting me.

I have many friends and damn it feels really amazing to have so much support. One of my greatest accomplishments in life is creating a beautiful support system. I had ample opportunity to become a bitter person who thought the worst of everyone, but I fucking fought not to be ruined by my aunt and my trauma.

Obviously, I still have some shit to work through like my easily triggered anger, claustrophobia, sudden touch, and general state of anxiety, but I think I'm pretty great. *Right?* Yeah. I'm fucking awesome.

Roman's name lights up the screen of my phone, telling me he's calling to video chat. *Interesting.* The positivity about myself brightens my mood and encourages me to answer his call.

Grinning, I lift the phone and start greeting him. "To what do I owe—"

The person who cuts me off shocks me and immediately brings tears to my eyes. "How could you?!"

Derrick fills the screen, fighting mad as he paces the length of a cozy living room. I've never seen Jared's dad so angry before, and it worries me quite a bit. He has a lot more gray in his hair than he did eleven years ago, and even after the accident Jared told me about, Derrick still has his athletic build. *Good for him.*

"I always knew you boys made a mistake when that sweet girl stopped coming around! And to hear that you believed what those assholes said about Erica holding you back from greatness?!"

Derrick's words make me sit up and pay attention. *Holy shit, he's talking about me.* And *swearing!*

"Jared, you know I'm proud of you, but it isn't like you grew up to be the president! How could Erica have ruined the possibility of you becoming a teacher?!"

Jared's not in the frame, but I still hear him. "I know, Dad."

"And you three never even aspired to be actors, or be in high-profile positions, or whatever!" Derrick cuts a hand through the air. "Yet, your parents whispered in your ear just enough to blind you of the future *YOU* wanted?!"

Oh shit.

"News flash, dipshits, words don't have the power to blindfold you. Erica made you all smile. She made you want to be *more*! How could you let the words of rich pricks steal your motivation?!"

"Derrick, honey..."

My breath catches, and I slam a hand over my mouth as a sob fights to break free. Jared's mom steps into view, and my goodness, she is *beautiful*. I wish I could reach through the phone and beg her to hug me.

I miss Clara so much.

Derrick seems to deflate, and the phone wiggles a little. Roman getting nervous maybe? Why does that make me feel giddy again?

When Derrick finally says something, his voice is much quieter. "Where is she?"

"What?" Jared, I think, asks.

"Erica. Where is she?" Derrick doesn't even turn to look near the guys. Just stares at the ground.

"Home, I think," Roman answers this time. I so badly want to scream that I'm here and beg for their address. What I wouldn't give to see Derrick's beaming smile as he greets me like he used to. These people were always so happy to see me. Would they still feel the same way?

"And what are your intentions?" Derrick's dropping bombs, I see.

The phone jolts, and I believe Roman just stiffened. *What is it he's worried about me hearing?*

Someone clears their throat. "To love and cherish her." Silence. At least on their end because I am absolutely *wheezing* over Felix's declaration. I can't catch my breath I am so stunned.

"We want her to be ours," Declan adds, and there are a few grunts that sound like agreement.

Derrick turns slowly, looking at a few different points around where Roman holds his phone. "Her presence is required at Thanksgiving. Fix it, bring her home."

The screen wiggles and the video chat ends, but my mind isn't ready to rest. *What just happened?! COME BACK!*

My phone pings, and a text from Roman comes through.

Roman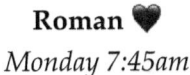
Monday 7:45am

Roman 🖤: Have a good day, beautiful.

Me: You too!

Read

Tuesday 6:56pm

Roman 🖤: Feeling avenged, Petal?

Tears soak my cheeks. Yes, and all I want to do is drive to their townhome and beg them to tell me if what they said was the truth. Which feels like a problem I should think about. Where did this attachment come from?

I *need three to five business days to process this.*

Thirty-Six

ROMAN

No response, only a read receipt. I would give anything to know what Blue thinks about the total ass-reaming Jared's dad gave us. Mr. Jones has always been the kindest man. I knew we would be in some deep shit when he found out about Blue, but I didn't expect *that*.

Derrick acted as if his own daughter, his flesh and blood, was the one so viscerally betrayed by us. Jared didn't seem surprised, neither did Declan, which makes me wonder what I missed after moving away.

"Roman, are you okay?" Declan murmurs. The other two left the kitchen a little while ago, but Dec stayed and seems to be watching over me. Sometimes I forget I'm the big brother.

That's what depression will do to a man.

I sigh, not at my brother but because of my negative thoughts. After checking the banana bread, I close the oven and lean against the counter. "I'm fine, D. Are you?"

He grunts and takes a swig of his beer. "He was right." I hate seeing him so troubled, but we deserved everything we got tonight.

"Obviously. But which part are you talking about?"

I would laugh at my brother's contemplative expression, but I'm feeling the same. There were a lot of truth bombs that exploded in our faces tonight. I think we're all struggling to see clearly again.

Declan fiddles with the rim of his can, seemingly getting his thoughts in order. "Erica, well Blue, really did make us strive to be the best we could possibly be."

Very true.

He continues. "I was always thinking about the best way to communicate without triggering her and learning how to make her smile. Our friendship taught me to be thoughtful and think of someone other than myself, you know?"

"I know."

Rage twists his features, not surprising me. "But that's so fucking stupid because while I thought I was far beyond my years with my *thoughtfulness*, I hurt her. I started only thinking about myself again!"

My big brother role perks up. "And what did you learn?"

Declan snorts a humorless laugh and finishes off his beer. "That loyalty shouldn't be blind. It's fucking earned. Not the result of blood relations. And Erica Bennett earned our loyalty. Not those pricks who created our sorry asses."

Amen. I open my mouth to agree when the back sliding glass door slams open, then a flash of Blue speeds past the kitchen and plants herself between us, the living room and the stairs.

"FELIX MOREL! Get out here right the fuck now!!"

Declan and I stand frozen, not wanting to draw attention to ourselves when there's a pissed off woman in our home. And not just any pissed off woman, but one who has every fucking right to rip our balls from our dicks.

"Jesus..." Declan whispers, sounding shocked and slightly terrified.

"FELIX!"

"Damn it, Blue!" Felix bellows, his stomps echoing from the back hallway. "My eardrums are going to bleed if you keep that up. What's your problem?!"

"YOU!" She stomps her foot, making her messy blue waves jump around her shoulders. "How could you say you want to *cherish* me and *love* me, when you never gave me an ounce of your loyalty?!"

Shit on sticks. Felix's frown is funny for half a second before he questions how the hell she heard him say that not three hours ago. *Fuck, it's getting late.*

"Roman called me, so I heard the whole thing."

Blue crosses her arms, looking sassy and ready to fight. The baggy shirt she's wearing over leggings does nothing to take away from her sexiness right now. Her bare feet are a little concerning considering I'm pretty sure it's illegal to drive barefoot.

Declan makes a strangled noise and turns to me at the same time Felix's glare moves from Blue to me with scary precision. Blue saves me from having to explain myself.

"Don't look at him, look at me!"

"Believe me, sweetheart, I'll gladly look at you all day long." *Why is Felix teasing her right now? She's pissed.*

"Damn," Declan groans quietly and adjusts himself. I roll my eyes but tune back in to the heated scene on the other side of the dining room table.

"Stop, Felix. Just stop," Blue grinds out. "I don't want that. I can't give you any more than I already have. There's nothing left!"

Felix frowns and steps toward her. "What does that mean?"

Blue steps back and stiffens. "That means I can't be in a relationship with you because you broke my trust!"

Felix *explodes,* his hands yanking on his hair as he faces off with the girl from our past. The woman we want to be our future.

"I'm sorry! *So fucking sorry!* We hate ourselves when we wake up each day. We despise the choices we made every night. Our parents took advantage of young minds who grew up with so much money all we knew was privilege! Day in and day out we were told we had to succeed to be loved. Once they planted that fucking seed, they told us all the ways we could ruin our lives! Approval was everything. Approval was survival. Loving a girl with a different upbringing and wanting to pursue an unconventional relationship with her was a surefire way to lose everything we grew up striving for!"

"What about loyalty?!" Blue fires back.

Felix steps forward again. "What about craving approval and love that seems just out of reach?!"

"Your friends approved of you. The people who spent their free time with you loved you. *I* loved you, dumbass."

I inch forward when I notice Felix's jaw clenching. *She triggered him.* Pride and relief make me a little light-headed when Felix handles the situation maturely.

"Blue," he warns, taking a shuddering deep breath, but his chest keeps heaving. "Watch the way you talk to me. Be pissed, swear, yell, whatever, but under no circumstances will I let you stand there and call us names in *our* home after ten at night."

Blue sucks in a small breath and Felix adds, "I've hit my quota for patience today. Don't push me on this one fucking thing. Please."

"He said please," Declan gasps way too fucking loud, so I elbow him in the ribs. My heart is pounding, and I feel sick watching their pain bleed out of their mouths in remembrance of our poor decisions. Blue glances back at us, but she refocuses on Felix.

"I'm sorry," she offers softly to which Felix nods. "A relationship with you guys won't work," she reiterates, sounding sad and a little cautious now. "I have Violet to think about and a career I'm working toward. Plus," she fidgets, breaking eye contact, "there's just way too much hurt. I won't get past everything that happened."

My gut clenches uncomfortably as if her words triggered my fight, flight, or freeze response. Does she really believe we caused her too much hurt to consider anything beyond this shallow friendship we've built? Sometimes I feel like she's holding back intentionally, so maybe if we keep pushing her...

"We won't give up," Jared declares, standing from the couch.

My brother jumps a little. *Has he always been this annoying?* "Was he there the whole time?"

"Yeah," I mutter. "Did you not see him peeking over the cushions?" Fucker looked like a scared child about to get yelled at for not doing the dishes before his mom got home.

Declan shushes me, and I have to hold back from shoving him. *What the hell?*

Blue crosses her arms, but her stance is different this time. Instead of guarding her chest, her forearms wrap around her waist. "I can't make you stop trying, but please hear me when I tell you that you broke me. I'm not that same girl. I'm not Erica anymore."

Yet, she's still my petal.

"And I don't do relationships," she adds hastily.

Like the manic idiot he is, Declan claps his hands to gain her attention. "What about pizza?" he asks with a grin wiggling our box of takeout.

Almost immediately, Blue brightens. "Oh! Yes, please. I'm starving."

Everyone seems to relax, and I question how smart my brother really is. He just diffused the situation with one suggestion. Maybe he's not as immature as I thought he was.

My timer for the banana bread dings, lighting a fire in my veins as Blue takes a slice of meat lover's pizza. *Fight activated.* I won't stop fighting for the girl.

Thirty-Seven

BLUE

"Y ou deserve everything you want, Ma. If that's them, then that's okay because it won't be like the first time. Sure, you're older and learned hard life lessons, but you are different. Plus, you've built a kick ass friend group who will always be looking out for you should you need to hide a body, or bodies."

Violet's words this morning have sparked many ideas and possible paths. I feel like it's up to me how my relationships with the guys progress, even as they force their way into every facet of my life.

It's tradition for me and Violet to go out for breakfast on our birthdays, and this year was no different except our topics of conversation. Normally I give boy advice and offer encouraging words, but the tables turned.

V watched me with a knowing expression while I stared at my hash browns for probably far too long. I just haven't been able to get them out of my head. *The guys, not the hash browns.*

Once again, after our emotions came to a head in a heated argument between me and Felix, they've only gotten closer to me. It's so hard not to think of myself as weak for allowing them in. Beating myself up about it doesn't help anything, though. They haven't allowed me space to pull away.

I tried the night Felix proclaimed their intentions to Jared's parents. It didn't do anything except bolster their resolve. And dampened my panties when Felix demanded respect.

Sometimes I lose myself in my feelings. I'm emotionally competent enough to know that I spent so long trying to tamp them down and focus on Violet that I caused a problem.

Avoiding my feelings just shoves them into a corner until they explode. And Felix handled me perfectly. He could have called me a bitch or told me I was being childish, or whatever, but he calmly told me he was out of patience and needed me to back off or leave.

What was shocking in its own right was that I didn't leave. It didn't even cross my mind, and that was just another sign that I might be losing the fight to keep my boundaries in place.

I kind of want to blame my friends for not bullying me into staying bitter and mean. Like right now, on my birthday of all days, they're doing the same thing as Violet.

Fucking supporting me.

I wholeheartedly believe I need a kick in the ass to

pull up my angry bitch panties so I can kick those fuckers to the curb. Yet here I am sipping a vodka seven with a lime while even *Janine* gives me the green light to follow my heart.

At least she seems to be choking on her words a little.

I need another drink, and music loud enough I can't hear the sappy shit my friends have to say.

The music's thumping, the shots are pouring, and I'm finally feeling free of everything. Maybe it's the alcohol or it could be the conversations I was forced to have before coming to Serpent's Kiss, but I'm feeling lighter than ever before.

Maybe it's knowing that no matter what choices I make, even possibly the wrong ones, my friends will still be there for me. It's strange to confide in others and care what they think, but I've had a few years to get used to it, I suppose.

Sweat begins to bead beneath my tiny blue dress as I grind to the beat of the music with my girls. *Nothing will ever compare to this feeling.*

A hand snakes around my chest from behind and draws me back into a large chest. I stiffen slightly, attempting to assess the situation when a rough voice shouts near my ear, but not close enough to feel intimate or sexy.

"Hey...boss."

I gasp, my heart flying to my throat as my hands reach for Kevin's forearm. *No way!* Bending back and to the side, I beam up at my friend and widen my eyes in question.

"You fucking did it, Blue!" he confirms, looking so damn proud my heart swells like a million fucking sizes. "Work out the logistics with Felix, then you'll get your own office!"

"You'll be taking orders from me by the end of the month!" I screech, jumping before flinging myself into one of his bear hugs.

I passed the security test, fitness test, and crazy ass interview our owner required to see how I would run things. It's crossed my mind that the owner demanded more from me because I'm a woman with no prior experience. It's fine, though, because it helped build my confidence for the position.

I couldn't have done it without Kevin's guidance on the important things in our building, nor could I have learned the required self-defense moves without Levi. My girl friends supported me from the beginning when I told them I wanted to manage our security team.

"I did it!"

Suddenly, Kevin is shoved away from me and replaced with an angry Jared. I'm too stunned to stop Jared from acting like an ass. "Get your fucking hands off my woman!"

Caveman much?

"Jared!" I grab his forearm and tug him toward me. "Stop."

The strobe lights flashing over his dark complexion mesmerize me as his brown eyes drag down to me. "He was holding you," Jared accuses with a slight snarl in his throat.

Maybe I should be annoyed with his behavior, but all I see is a kind of possessiveness I've been craving for a long ass time. *Am I crazy?*

Dragging him down to me by his neck so I can speak in his ear, I shiver when his slight stubble scratches my cheek. "That's Kevin," I say. "Levi's husband."

Jared pulls back a little to study my face, and I let him see the truth in my eyes. I haven't fucked around with any man since they came back into my life and frazzled all my nerve endings. His gaze softens with curiosity and *adoration?*

Unable to hold the good news in any longer, I clutch his neck harder and yell out my victory. "I got the job! I'm going to be the security manager!"

Excitement widens his gaze, and his hands grip my hips in a tight hold. "I'm so fucking proud of you!"

Where my heart swelled with Kevin's praise, my soul *ignites* with Jared's. Before I can thank him or melt into a puddle of tears, he yanks me into his solid body and presses his lips to mine.

I gasp, opening up to allow him entry. Music and booze freed me before; now it's just Jared. He unshackles me with every squeeze of his fingers, every nip of his teeth, and tease of his tongue.

Music doesn't exist here.

The other bodies writhing on the dance floor disappear.

Just me and Jared. The boy who hurt me, now the man who ignites me.

Until it isn't just us. Heat scorches my back and new hands wrap themselves beneath my hip bones. "My turn," Roman rumbles in my ear, soaking my pussy.

Rome tugs me away from Jared, breaking the kiss and starting a new fire in me as he trails his own path of nips and licks up the side of my neck.

Holy shit...

Thirty-Eight

FELIX

She. Is. Something. I don't think defining Blue with words is possible. She has something that few people have.

It's an energy. One that no matter how hard you try to avoid it or deny its existence, it captures you anyway. Once it has you, you wonder why you fought it to begin with.

She draws you in, and once she so much as smiles at you, you'll never want to be free of her orbit.

Blue Bennett is life. How would you describe life?

Life is...

Beautiful, dark, chaotic, scary, wonderful, maybe even a little unpredictable? And you know what? No matter how unbalanced the scales can get sometimes between the good and bad, you still fucking *crave it.* Want more of it. Beg for more time with it. Worship it.

Blue is...

Beautiful, dark, chaotic, scary, wonderful, and a little unpredictable. And I know for a fact, no matter the good days or bad days, I *crave* her. I want more of her. To beg for her time. I want to worship her.

So if I had to describe Blue, I would tell you she has an energy that matches *life*.

Her face is lit up like the sun, while her body grinds like sin. Arms lifted over Roman's shoulders, she looks larger than life and like she won't ever stop reaching for the stars.

One year older.

I vow right here and now never to miss another birthday.

"We should get her home," Declan suggests, having chosen to stay mostly sober with me. I wouldn't have minded if he had a few more drinks, but I'm proud of him for setting a boundary for himself.

As the designated driver, I've spent the past few hours watching over the group and making them drink water. Declan has been taunting me with not-so-subtle dick touches, making my job to look out for everyone a bit harder.

Like right now!

"Felix?" he moans in my ear and slides his hand up my shirt.

I clench my jaw and grab his like I love to do. Canting his head to the side, I growl out my demand, "Get your ass to the break room. If you aren't on your knees when I get there, you aren't coming for a fucking week."

He chokes on a gasp and calls me rude. That's what teases get. I watch him push through the crowd, and once he's out of sight, I hustle for Kevin and Levi.

Their heads are close together at the bar, but they listen adamantly when I ask them to keep watch for me. I don't mind their knowing smirks because I'm all in on Declan.

I have no embarrassment or shame about our budding relationship. He's mine, just like Blue is—will be.

I'm thankful for my jeans keeping my boner at bay, but once I bust through the door to the staff lounge, I'm ready to rip the fabric from my body. Snarling and popping the button, I lock the door behind me.

"Impatient much?"

My blood heats in response to Declan's sassy remark. I turn and stomp toward his kneeling form just feet away from me.

"You're gonna suck my cock to keep your sassy mouth quiet, and while you're at it, you're going to fuck your wandering hand."

He raises a dark brow and smirks up at me. He must either be as impatient as me or realize just how fucking serious I am because he reaches for my crotch.

My breathing turns ragged as he undoes my jeans. His large hand pulls me free, and I sigh in relief only for my lungs to stutter when he sucks me down his throat in one move.

"Fuck," I hiss. His hair is in my fist a moment later. Unable to control myself, I dominate his mouth until he's gagging and drooling out the sides. Cursing again, I pause and nudge his hip with my foot to get him moving on his own cock.

He moans and flicks his gaze up to me. While my

balls draw up in appreciation for the sexy man on his knees, my heart thumps extra hard because he's *Declan*. *My* Declan now.

"Make yourself feel good, D. But don't forget about me," I remind him and drag the head of my cock along his tongue again.

I have to shift a little to watch him jerk himself off, and that movement makes him swallow around me. Tensing, I try to pull him off. "Dec, you do that again and I'll come. Wait a second."

Of course, he doesn't wait. Declan swallows, then gags, effectively sending me right over the edge into unimaginable pleasure. "Fuck fuck fuck!" I roar out my release, and manage to catch the final spurts of his own release painting his white T-shirt.

Unable to help myself, I yank him to his feet, catch him when he stumbles and force my tongue into his mouth. Satisfaction and something primal expand in my chest when Declan clings to me and steals the breath from my lungs as if I am his oxygen.

I pull away first even though I hate breaking our moment that went from sexy to tender really quick. "We need to get Blue and the guys home. Then maybe..." I gulp, not used to seeking out *more* from someone. "We sleep together tonight? Not sex," I add, knowing we agreed to wait until Blue was with us. "Just cuddling."

Ugh, that was so lame.

Declan kisses away my embarrassment then says, "I'd love that."

Me too.

Thirty-Nine

BLUE

Bacon. All hail the motherfucking bacon.

The only reason I'm dragging my ass out of bed right now is because of the mouthwatering scent of breakfast. My head pounds, but it has nothing on the grumbling of my belly.

Did I drink on an empty stomach?

Hangover headache aside, I'm fine. The urge to vomit hasn't risen, I'm not still stumbling, and I remember everything from last night. I may have made out with Jared on the dance floor and dirty danced with Roman, but I at least put my foot down when Declan offered to tuck me in last night.

They all walked my giggling self up to my apartment. Violet was waiting up with a cheeky little grin on her face when she saw all four of them follow me inside. Once she made sure I was home safe, she went to pick up Bethany, Janine, and Dakota from the club too.

Gosh, I love her.

What I don't recall is anything after I wished them goodnight, forced myself through the shower, and passed the fuck out. For once I was able to sleep all the way through my sexy dreams which was an awesome birthday treat.

I rush through pulling some cozy shorts up my legs beneath my baggy T-shirt and quickly brush my teeth. Glancing at my hair, I decide the ratted mess would be better pulled back into a bun. All squared away with a ball of fuzzy socks in my hand, I start to the kitchen.

Deep voices that definitely do not belong to Violet make me slow down and lighten my steps. *Did the guys spend the night?*

"Listen, kid..." I was right. It's Roman. "I'm not teaching you that until Blue gives the okay."

Now in my line of sight, I watch Violet cross her arms and square off with him. "I'm not a kid. I'm eighteen, and Blue won't care."

"Violet," Roman sighs, looking lost and a little frustrated on the other side of the kitchen table as V. "I know your Ma and there's no way she'd allow this."

My heart simultaneously flips and warms at hearing Roman call me Ma. Not only is that a representation of his acceptance of Violet in my life, but I can also see Roman as a dad now. Firm, kind, and a little bewildered at all the questions.

Wait, why do I care if he would be a good father?

Violet twists in her chair and addresses the shirtless man making bacon in my kitchen. "Felix, what do you think?"

I lean against the wall because I'm damn curious

about what's happening out here. My eyebrows jump to my forehead when Felix's shoulder start bouncing and a laugh sounds through the apartment.

"Sorry, sunshine. I'm not getting in the middle of...what was it?"

I swear I can feel Violet rolling her eyes. "Round-house kick. And you wouldn't be my practice dummy. Just tell Roman to teach me."

Oh wow, now she's pouting. Sometimes I forget she's still only eighteen. A soft snore draws my attention to the living room where Declan and Jared are splayed out on the floor in a makeshift bed of blankets and throw pillows.

Jesus, they really did sleep over.

Felix turns around, spatula in hand, and pins my kid with a look. "How 'bout you start with simple moves? That one is too dangerous for beginners."

She sucks in a breath, and I know exactly what's about to happen. Violet's had her fair share of training and moments where she's actually had to use her knowledge, which is a touchy subject. Felix just pissed her off.

"I know enough about self-defense. If Roman would just—"

"I said no," Felix states firmly. Honestly I'm a bit surprised about how many toes he's stepping on.

"You aren't my dad!" Violet all but shouts, making me cringe. I should step in. But if they want to be with me, then they need to figure out their own way to deal with Violet's behavior. V has a lot of trauma. While she is happy, outgoing, smart, and motivated, she has triggers, and she's still young.

"Violet," Roman says softly, drawing her fiery attention to him. "I never said no. I'd like to make sure Blue is okay with me teaching you that move because *I'm* not comfortable without her permission. This isn't about your capabilities or me trying to control you."

Violet deflates and murmurs what I hope is an apology. Taking that as my cue, I exit the hallway and beeline right for the bacon. To Felix, who's looking at me with a heated expression, I whisper, "Now you tell her your point of view."

He swallows, looking me up and down before addressing the situation. "I have a thing about safety and respect. One, I didn't want you learning something that could hurt you. Two, you weren't respecting Roman's decision when you asked me to force him into something he didn't want to do. I apologize for being too direct and snappy with you, sunshine."

She doesn't hesitate. "I'm sorry too," Violet's voice wobbles a little, and I know she's anxious to mend these new bonds she's forming. "To you and Roman."

The bacon in my mouth struggles to go down as I swallow when Roman gets up and pulls V into a side hug.

"You okay?" Felix asks, tucking a strand of hair behind my ear. All I do is nod, because *wow*, what a morning already. "Where'd you get that shirt, sweetheart?"

Confused by his question while being distracted by

Declan and Jared standing and stretching in my living room, I stutter. "Wh-What?"

"I said," he presses into my side with a heated look on his face, "where did you get this shirt?"

"Oh...I actually don't know." Where *did* I find it?

"Hey!" Declan shouts, eyeing me like he wants to eat me. "Is that my favorite fucking shirt from junior year?!"

Oh shit! "Oh my god! I totally forgot! I took this after we did that hike in the pouring rain!"

How could I forget? I was freezing, and when we got back to the car, Declan offered me his extra shirt in the back. I never gave it back.

"Do you want it back?" I ask hesitantly. This is *my* favorite shirt.

Declan saunters over to me, loops an arm around my back and shakes his head. "It's all yours. Just like we are," he adds and presses his lips to mine so fast I don't even have the chance to close my eyes.

Violet saves me from his delicious touch and suggestive words with her own demand. "I need all four of you guys in a line, kay? I'll teach you a new viral dance that my followers will *love*. Then after that, someone can teach me to do a roundhouse kick."

I laugh, rush over to her and kiss the top of her head. "I'll teach you, V. Don't worry."

Her wide-eyed look of shock lights up my morning. I love surprising her. My four men surprise *me* not half an hour later when they've completed the dance perfectly. And so damn sexy. Especially when they continue feeding me bacon and fruit.

Wait...*my* four men?!

Forty

JARED

"So her cousin makes money by posting videos of herself dancing and hiking online?"

Snorting into my lasagna, I truly cannot help but laugh at my mom's bewildered expression. Declan, of course, is biting back his own laughter too. Felix watches me and Declan, daring us to ruin the evening.

My mom, dad, and sister are over for dinner tonight, and it's only been a little tense. We haven't seen them since they found out the truth about Blue a few weeks ago.

I couldn't stand them being angry with me any longer, so I invited them, and like the kind people they are, they came. Mom still hugged me, Dad slapped me on the shoulder a little too hard, and my sister, Nichole, would barely look at me.

Knowing how I disappointed them and hurt my family fucking sucks. It's been feeding into my never-ending guilt for years, but like the scared son I am, I was terrified for them to know how much I really fucked up.

This wasn't one of those times I admitted I used to sneak out a lot in high school, and we laugh it off. No, I damaged something when the truth finally came out. Be it their trust in me or the way they see me, it's a gut punch either way.

"Don't ask me why or how it works," Roman replies to my mom. "Blue's in a lot of Violet's content. Most of it, actually. They're cute."

And far too sexy. Watching Blue roll her body and pop her ass out in short shorts online is not my favorite fucking thing to see. Felix grunts, and I'd bet money he's thinking the same thing I am. Way too many people watched my woman flip pancakes in tiny sleep shorts that barely peeked beneath her sweatshirt this morning.

The number of views I saw on it bothered the shit out of me, and I refuse to think about some of the comments.

"Why did she change her name?" Mom looks afraid of the answer she's going to get, and she probably should be. This will hurt.

"She said..." Roman begins but swallows repeatedly as if the words won't come out.

I jump in, because I should be the one to tell my family. "She said Erica died a long time ago."

The impact of my words has my dad's head falling forward, Mom gasping with her hand to her mouth, and Nichole pushing away from the table. I would like to ask my sister where she's going and what she's thinking, but by the time I actually gather the courage, she's slamming the back door.

"What—" Mom gulps and looks at my dad a few times before asking her question. "Do you know what happened to her after she moved?"

"Why? Do you know something?" Declan wonders, looking a little sick and concerned.

Dad lifts his head and glares at Declan. "What do you mean? Obviously, we don't know because you kids hid this from us. And also, how the hell do *you* not know yet?"

"I—" Declan stutters, not having an answer to a very good question.

"Derrick," Roman interjects, "Blue isn't very forthcoming with information about herself. We're trying not to push her away."

"And have you monopolized your time by trying to show and tell her how you've changed?" Dad accuses very accurately, so we remain silent. He sighs and pushes his plate away—I've never seen my dad decline a good meal. "Boys, her telling you a part of her *died* is really big."

Defensiveness roars to life in my bones. "We know that, Dad."

He pins me with a look. "Have you paid attention to her behavior? Does anything upset her? I'm worried there may have been abuse with how horrible her aunt was and the men she brought over."

Roman cocks his head and leans forward. "What do you mean by *upset her*?"

"Triggers, honey," my mom specifies. "Does she

flinch? Hate the dark? Does she dislike anything that might clue you in to what happened and how you might be able to support her?"

My dad nods. "The sooner you pick up on the things that make her nervous, the sooner you'll earn her trust and be her safe space."

"She freaked out in the car when we had the child locks on," I remind the guys, ready to figure this out.

"You locked her in the fucking car?" Dad grits out, sounding absolutely livid.

I ignore him because I'm on a roll now. "She startles easily. When I snuck up on her at the liquor store, she dropped her wine, and it shattered. Then Felix, you grabbed her arm when she wasn't looking, and the same thing happened."

Felix nods with a pinched expression. "She got so angry...then basically begged us to leave her alone." He groans and stares up at the ceiling. "Have we been triggering her without even knowing it since then?"

We're silent until Declan admits, "Yeah. If I approach her too fast, it's like her flight response kicks in, and she steps back. She flinches every time I touch her when she doesn't see it coming."

Roman adds his two cents. "I've noticed how antsy she gets. She doesn't like to stay in one room for too long. Maybe that's because her aunt made them live in fucking shoeboxes?"

"I'm going to check on Nichole..." my mom mutters and leaves. Dad frowns after her and stands as well.

I follow suit. "Dad?"

He shakes his head and walks out of the kitchen.

Annoyed with his dismissal, I follow, ready to share my opinion like a dumbass. I stop short once I'm on the patio and the breath is yanked from my lungs.

"You're so beautiful!" Mom wails from our neighbor's patio, holding Blue's cheeks between her hands. Tears track down my girl's face as she stares into my mom's eyes with so much longing and sorrow.

I watch with my bleeding heart in my throat as Blue, the woman I love and betrayed, absolutely *crumbles* in my mother's embrace.

I lose sight of Blue and my mom when Dad wraps his arms around them. My own eyes burn, and my choked sob is muffled by theirs.

Who knew witnessing a reunion so beautiful could hurt so fucking much?

Forty-One

BLUE

My mind is a mess. I've been struggling to rein in my train of thought for days, and nothing's working. Bethany suggested I meditate, but there's something about meditation that raises the hell out of my anxiety.

Cleaning and listening to Linkin Park is the closest I've gotten to peace. Then Violet shows her pale face, making me worry all over again. I don't know what the hell is going on with her, and I most certainly have no idea how to find out.

I've asked all the normal parent questions like, are you okay, is someone bothering you, do you need to tell me anything? She gives me short answers and comes back later acting like everything is normal.

There's something going on, and my gut is screaming at me to figure it out. To fix it. Yet, my brain is telling me Violet needs space to figure it out on her own. She's a legal adult. It's time to let her catch herself sometimes.

I fucking hate it.

How do I manage this? I'm basically a single mom with adjusted boundaries and expectations because I'm not *actually* her mom.

After seeing Jared's parents the other night, I'm dying to ask Jared for his mom's phone number. I need advice from a mother who loves with her whole heart.

When I was sharing a bottle of wine with Beth by her gas fire pit, the last person I expected to see was Nichole. She looked so guilty and sad that I didn't hesitate to hug her.

We were friends before I realized who she was related to—we still are. I apologized for avoiding her because in no way is any of this her fault. I've said it before and I'll say it again I'm the worst sometimes.

Then Clara, Jared's wonderful mother, gasped and rushed toward me. She called me beautiful, but I couldn't help wondering what she truly thought of me. And as much as it hurt, that made me wonder what my own mom would think of me if she were still alive.

There was so much sorrow and excitement over seeing Jared's parents that it wasn't until after they left that I began questioning things. Like why didn't they reach out to me if they were worried about me like they said they were?

I did find out from Clara that the guys never told them anything. Basically, just that we weren't friends anymore. But still my feelings are hurt, which seems unfair to put on them.

Clara and Derrick were put in an odd position when

their son minimized what happened, so why would they ask for my phone number and check on me?

Would I do the same thing with Violet's friends? Actually...*have I?!*

I can't fight the groan that slips free as I rub my eyes. *This* is what I'm talking about. My brain goes off on random ass tangents which feel important but aren't in the moment.

The pressure behind my eyes and into more forehead builds as I try to rub away the ache. There's too much going on.

"Blue..." A soft touch tickles my bare elbow, sending shivers across my skin. "Come sit down, babe." Declan's voice is so soft tears spring to my eyes.

I don't even check the counter for the latte I've been waiting on. Instead, I follow Declan blindly to a cozy booth and slide in. The weight of everything settles on my chest, making it hard to breathe. *Stress.*

Declan's saying something, but all I can focus on is the coffee cup he slides in front of me. *He's being so nice.*

Do I deserve this kindness? Am I making life harder for everyone?

More voices join, but I'm already spiraling like I have been for days.

Roman, Declan, Jared, and Felix hurt me. They *hurt* me. Their impact on my life was worse than Aunt Linda's abusive boyfriends. How can I forgive that?

Do I plan to? If I don't even after all the effort they're putting in to make things right between us, does that make me selfish?

I am *definitely* making shit harder for everyone, and it makes me feel like a hypocrite. How can I continue to punish them when I know how much it hurts to be made to feel like you aren't enough?

Everything they've been doing...Has it been enough?

My belly twists uncomfortably. *Will their efforts ever be enough to outweigh the pain they caused?*

How am I supposed to decide that, though?! The unfairness of my predicament makes me angry and irrational.

They ghosted me. *They* left me when I needed them. Why in the hell is it up to *me* to make this decision? It feels like for my entire life, everything has been on me.

This is just another fucking decision I have to make. I want to scream at them and tell them to fuck off, but those are my scars talking. I'd rather forgive them and collapse into a puddle of tears in their arms because my heart feels like she deserves their love.

My mind questions whether I can trust their affection and *loyalty*. Ugh, that word is so fucking tainted now.

And my soul? She's weary and tired. There are too many voices and feelings tugging me every which way.

How am I supposed to decide? *What* am I supposed to decide? If they've redeemed themselves? If they've grown enough? Do I *believe* they're redeemable? Maybe the answers aren't factual but personal. What if...what if instead of judging *them* and their actions, I focus inward and assess my feelings?

"Blue Bennett, you're scaring the shit out of us."

I blink. Felix's sharp tone snaps me out of my epiphany. I'm shocked to see Jared and Declan sitting on the other side of the booth with worried expressions. Roman's beside me, his thigh almost touching mine. And Felix has his fists braced on the table, glaring down at me.

Licking my lips, I fidget nervously. *What is wrong with me?* "Sorry, what did you say?"

"Is everything okay?" Felix grits out, looking like he wants to say more, but Declan's soft touch on his hand calms him.

My initial reaction is to nod, but there's no way the guys will let me off the hook if I brush it off. Sighing, I tuck my hair over one shoulder. "I'm stressed. Work is changing, which is great, but still a lot. You guys are everywhere." I gesture to the current setting. I'm not even quite sure why they're all here. A bit ago, I had come down to Declan's café for a latte, and suddenly they're all here?

Roman lays his hand on my thigh, the heat warming me to my core. "You walked in while we were here having breakfast."

"Oh..." I gulp, wondering what they must think about my obvious issues this morning. "Well, anyway. Violet's been acting strange for a few weeks now, and I don't know how to help her."

"Weird how?" Jared asks.

"Closed off, jumpy, defensive..." I list, but I'm unable to fully explain the *feeling* I have that something is going on.

Declan opens his mouth and snaps it shut. "What?" I ask, wanting any kind of advice.

Dec shakes his head. "I was going to ask if you've looked through her phone, then I remembered she's an adult and that would be weird."

My shoulders slump. *Fuck.* I'd love to, but not only would that be horribly wrong, I also don't think I want to know what's on there.

Half a thought forms that would be best not to say, but the scars are talking now. "So, I think it's best if..." I trail off. Felix narrows his eyes at me, making me cringe a little, but I keep going. "I think it's best if we go our separate ways—"

"Absolutely not," Felix snaps, slamming his fist down on the table with a dull thump.

The tears that had disappeared before start anew. Why does pushing them away feel so wrong? "I need to focus on Violet. I need to be there for her, Felix."

"We aren't going anywhere. We will be here for *both* of you. Don't you dare push us away." His expression is steel, and his gaze is like fire. "You and Violet will be coming over for weekly dinners from here on out."

My rebuttal melts away as my heart warms. "Okay," I whisper instead, allowing a few tears to fall which Roman wipes away.

Weak my scars accuse, but I just realized not five minutes ago that it's not about the guys. *Not really*. It's about me and what I'm feeling.

Having Felix fight for me, Roman comfort me, Jared being attentive, and Declan challenging me makes me...*happy*. Something in my foundation shifts and settles into place. Judging by the way I lean into Roman, and hold Jared's gaze without feeling nauseated, I'd venture to say my trust in them in building.

Trust. Happy.

Words I never thought I'd associate with these men ever again. I hope, really fucking hope, I can add *safe* to that list soon too.

Forty-Two

DECLAN

"Please help me," I beg my big brother as I rush into the kitchen. "I feel like I'm getting sick. Like I could throw up, and my hands are shaking."

Roman continues chopping a head of lettuce, but he glances at me and my trembling fingers with a furrowed brow. "When did this start?"

Thinking through the timeline of today proves to be a little harder than I thought. "I don't know. Right when we invited Blue and Violet over for dinner, maybe. Shit, do you think I'm contagious? Son of a bitch, after Blue's slight meltdown yesterday at my coffee shop, this could be her final straw if she gets sick.

"She's already so stressed out, and with her starting in security next week, I could fuck it all up with my nausea. Fuck, what if Blue throws up all over the monitors at work and ruins them?!"

I'm pacing now, thinking of every scenario in which I could fuck something up. Our presence in her life is meant to make things the opposite of worse. We want to prove to Blue that we're better, yes, but we also want to help her and bring her happiness.

I can't make life harder for Blue Bennett. I *won't*.

"You're anxious, man," Roman informs me with a slap on the back. His words and rough touch snap me out of my wayward thoughts.

"What?" I huff and cross my arms. "No. I don't get anxious. I'm cool, calm, and collected."

Roman snorts and brushes by me with a large bowl of salad. "No. That's Felix. You're chaotic and a little unhinged sometimes."

I open my mouth to retort, but the doorbell rings, and Jared comes flying by with a big grin aimed at me. "Roman's right!"

"Fuck off," I shout even as my friend disappears from view to greet Violet and Blue.

"Hey," my brother murmurs, coming over to me after setting the table, "What's bothering you?"

I slump, feeling defeated and slightly lightheaded. "I don't want to mess this up with either of them. Violet is Blue's other half. We have to make her like us, Rome."

Roman's thoughtful look turns into a bright smile as someone comes skipping into the room. "I think she already does," Roman whispers just as Violet comes into my view.

"What's up, bitches?!"

Maybe Roman's right. The blonde firecracker might actually enjoy our presence.

Conversation has been pretty light and surface level since the girls got here an hour ago. Not that I mind, especially considering I'm no longer in a slight state of panic.

We learned Violet doesn't plan on going to college any time soon, if ever, because she really loves being a content creator. We all just nodded our heads except for Jared who was incredibly interested in the statistics of success for that kind of work.

Blue watched Violet with so much warmth in her gaze that my love for her doubled in size. She's like a soft weight on my heart which Felix protects with something sharper, fiercer.

Violet was more than thrilled to tell us all about her most recent hikes across the US, and we enjoyed listening. Blue jumped in to add more detail and story since she joins Violet a few times a year as well.

I'm completely enthralled. Not only by Blue's slightly loose jeans and tight black T-shirt, but by the connection she has built with her cousin. Her *kid*, as they say.

Her blue hair also has a tussled curls vibe, and her makeup is subtle, giving off domesticated vibes. I yearn to tug her close and hold her to my chest.

Felix's hand flexes on my thigh when Blue tips her head back and laughs. I sigh reflexively in response to her joy and the length of her creamy skin. Now I'm eager to cuddle up next to her and leave a trail of kisses from her ear to her collarbone.

"So!" Violet claps, bouncing in her chair. I can't help but study the young girl for any signs of distress. She hasn't shown any of the behavior Blue has been worried about, but maybe Violet's just concealing her struggles really well.

After all, we're still kind of strangers to her.

Much to my amusement, Violet points her breadstick at me then circles it to encompass all of us. "What are you guys doing for Halloween?"

I frown. *Hmm.* I can feel Felix waiting for me to answer, and when I check to see if Jared or Roman have any ideas, they're scratching their chins. Normally we do something like decorate our place, get candy for the trick or treaters and go out for some drinks or see some live music.

"We haven't talked about it, actually. We've been a little..." I catch Blue's gaze and fucking *relish* in the widening of her eyes when I say, "distracted."

Violet hums and taps her fork on her mostly empty plate of potpie. "Ma and I go see scary movies at the theater together every Halloween. You all should come!"

Blue breaks our stare down to frown at her cousin. "Do I get a say, V?"

"Nope!" I interject, ready to play my chaotic role to get us even more embedded in Blue's life. "Violet invited us. No takebacksies."

Felix pinches my leg a little, making me gasp and

glare at him. He's not looking at me but at Violet with a soft expression. "We would love to come. Thank you, sunshine."

"Great!" Violet shouts and jumps from the table. "I don't mean to eat and run, but my friends are going on a hike, and I told them I'd join."

"What time will you be home?" Blue asks, looking nervous.

"Not sure," Violet admits and kisses the top of Blue's head. "You stay. I have someone waiting outside. Love you! Bye guys, thanks for dinner."

Just like that, Violet's gone in a whirlwind of blonde hair and enthusiasm. "Does she always have so much energy?" Roman wonders out loud.

Blue sighs and takes a small sip of her wine suddenly looking exhausted. "Yes. I don't remember the last time I slept in while she was home."

Roman nods like he understands and pulls her chair away from the table. He lifts Blue by the elbow and starts pulling her toward the couch. I'm shocked she doesn't fight him or say a word as he wraps a blanket around her.

"You stay here. Brownies will be done shortly. We'll clean up and come join you in a few minutes," Roman explains, pinning her with an intense stare.

I can see the side of her face as her expression pinches. Just as she's about to protest, Roman rubs his thumb across her cheek and begs, "Let us take care of you. Please."

She deflates, and as I load the dishwasher, I hope like hell we will have a lifetime of taking care of Blue.

Forty-Three

BLUE

It's fucking hot in here. Not the kind of heat that makes you sweat but the kind that makes your core boil. My tummy flutters with bubbles from the molten lava between my legs.

The tension in the room ramped higher and higher with each man who surrounded me on the living room sectional. When Roman asked me to relax and we'd watch a movie soon, a teeny red flag went off in my head that this might not be a good idea. But damn it felt nice to be taken care of for once in my fucking life.

The red flag that started waving around in my mind an hour ago has gotten much larger, brighter and far more frantic the wetter my pussy gets. *This is not a good idea.*

This being whatever my body is craving.

If I'm being completely honest, I don't know what Jared put on the TV. We're already forty-five minutes in and I haven't focused on the screen long enough to figure it out.

I don't care either. All I care about is Felix's mother-fucking hand moving beneath the blanket spread across his and Declan's lap. I hear nothing but the hitches in Declan's breathing.

The movie is *nothing* compared to the slow build of whatever those two are doing. Oh, I forgot to mention —Jared's *torturing* me. Maybe I should have protested when he sat so close to me, but there were a few inches then. Now, not so much. Literally none.

My body had a mind of its own when I pulled my knees up and rested them on Jared's thigh. Total mistake. He's warm and solid. His hand rests on my leg, fingers tickling the skin between the hole in my jeans.

I'm wet and pliable.

The wine loosened me up enough to put myself in this position, and the slight buzziness in my head keeps me from really paying attention to the red flag. *Caution, do NOT enter.*

I won't, but they—

Shifting, my nose catches a yummy whiff of Jared's sweatshirt and a little sigh exhales from my mouth. Mortification swamps me, and I duck into his arm a little. Roman's heavy gaze *still* lingers on me. I don't think he's seen more than a few minutes of the movie either.

I'm pleading with the universe to give me the boost I need to jump off this couch and leave, but it doesn't happen. I'm comfortable and incredibly fucking intrigued by the new sounds coming from the other corner of the sectional.

Unable to help myself, I glance over at the happy couple. My breath stutters out in response to Felix staring at me as his hand moves in a way that makes it *so painfully* obvious what he's doing to Declan.

Up and down the blanket shifts, and with my attention now completely on the movement, Felix speeds up and grins at me. *Asshole.*

Declan's volume rises until a deep groan slips out as his hips buck. Awareness slams into me, and I quickly check to see how Roman feels about his brother getting a handjob *right fucking there.*

Except, instead of finding disgust on Rome's face, he's nodding at Jared beside me. Roman relaxes back into his chair and spreads his legs to make space for— *holy shit*—his huge boner.

What the hell is happening?

"What's happening, Bee," Jared rumbles in my ear. *Shoot, I said that out loud.* "Is Felix is getting Declan off because you wound my friend up *way* too much today. He was all anxious about making you happy, then you waltzed in here looking sexy as fuck, ate our food we made for you, snuggled on our couch, and *relaxed.*"

What does that have to do with Roman currently taking his monster cock out of his pants?! "I'm not sure—"

Jared pulls my leg higher on his leg. "You riled Declan up. Roman's barely hanging on by a thread. Come on, haven't you noticed how antsy Dec has been since we sat down? Roman hasn't been able to stop staring at your gorgeous face. And I'm fighting not to dive my hands into your cute fucking jeans and rub your little clit until you come alongside my friends."

"I—" Shit, my heart is pounding, and I'm *stunned* by the sheer filth coming out of Jared's mouth. Plus, Declan and Roman look ready to come any second now.

Warm lips press against my temple, and I relax, not having noticed I tensed up. "I won't do more than watch you watch them if you don't want me to. Or I can drive you home right now. *Or*," Jared nips my earlobe, "I can make you feel so good, Bee."

Caution! Caution! Do NOT enter!

I'm ready to pull away because this is a really bad idea, but as I shift to do that, the seam of my jeans rubs against my clit. I gasp and cling to Jared, sensitivity and need forcing me to seek more.

"Okay," I breathe out, closing my eyes because I can't believe I'm about to do this.

Jared's hand disappears from my leg, and I figure he'll unbutton my jeans like he wants. Instead, he grabs my jaw and forces my head back. "You'll watch my friends while I touch you. Right, Bee?"

His eyes are so damn dark, and the dominance pouring off of him steals the agreement from my lips. "Yes. I–I'll watch."

He nods curtly. "Good. Now..." His tone softens as does his touch that trails from my face between my breasts and to my waistband. "Let me take care of you."

I feel my lips part at the same time my button unclasps. Heat trails from my belly and pools in my pulsing clit. Jared smiles, then presses the pads of his fingers and begins to rub the ache away.

My gasp is drowned out by Declan cursing. I snap my attention to the hot as fuck duo and my mouth goes absolutely dry. Dec clutches the armrest with one hand, and the other is beneath the blanket but seems to be extended onto Felix's lap.

Jesus. "Oh!" I squeak when Jared's finger reaches lower and swipes through my folds.

"Fuck, Bee. You're so wet. I wonder what you taste like."

"Jared," I groan and kick the blanket off of us, the heat actually making me sweat now. It's so hot, so sexy. I want *more*.

Caution. I arch, seeking everything Jared can do in the tight confines of my jeans.

Roman grunts, the sound feeling primal as my clit tingles for his deep voice. Watching him work his cock is like absolute magic.

"I'm-I'm close," I moan and fight not to squeeze my eyes shut as Jared focuses his attention on the spot I need him most.

"Fuck, Felix!" Declan bellows, throwing his own blanket off. He roars as his release explodes from his dick, coating his T-shirt in cum.

The sight of his pleasure and Felix's hot kiss on Declan's throat is so erotic my toes curl and my body stiffens. Then Roman grunts out my name, drawing my attention to his cock releasing ropes of cum.

I'm done for. "Oh shit. SHOOT!" The tension in my core becomes unbearable until it feels like it explodes in waves and waves of mind-numbing bliss. Jared works out each jolt of pleasure that rips through my body like a pro all the while he murmurs encouragement.

More kisses tingle my temple as Jared buttons my jeans. It feels nice and cozy, like I could sink into this feeling every day of my life. My eyes are closed as my body sinks. But I crash land right on a fidgeting red flag that's wondering if it's needed anymore.

I blew right past my own boundaries, and all I've found is a comfortability that scares me. As much as I want to stay curled up with them, I need space. "Can-Can you take me home now?" I ask Jared without opening my eyes. I feel the post-orgasmic coziness evaporate with my words. Uncomfortable with the guilt turning in my tummy, I look at them and say, "I'm not used to this. I just want some space...I'm not running, I promise."

"Space means thinking," Felix replies with a slight accusatory tone. I see beyond it, though. He's scared.

I smile softly in understanding. "I'm not running, I promise. Plus." I flutter my lashes at Jared. "I'm sleepy now."

Jared smirks with a mix of amusement and happiness. Lust still lingers in his gaze, but I ignore it. "I bet you're tired."

Heat rises to my cheeks, bringing me full circle. "Please drive me home?" I ask sweetly.

Without warning, Jared presses a gentle kiss to my lips and warms my heart with his next words. "As you wish, Bee."

Their hugs and soft kisses goodbye linger like a warm blanket all the way home just as Jared's hand on my thigh does. Of course, like the gentleman he's showing himself to be, Jared walks me up and into my apartment. He reminds me to lock the door behind him but not before he sears my tongue with a lasting makeout session that has me wishing I was ready for him to stay the night.

Not yet, but not *never*.

Forty-Four

ROMAN

No matter how many reps I do, I *cannot* center myself. I'm aware it has everything to do with a certain Bennett woman. She's everything, and I feel like nothing.

I'm not worthy of Blue and I don't know if I ever will be. The selfish, bone-deep need to prove myself to her just so I *might* be able to get the scraps has been a struggle.

There's never been a competition between me and the guys when it comes to Blue. We've always been on even ground probably because we're all so different. Jared and Declan may be outgoing, funny free spirits, but at their core they are amazing individuals.

Rep after rep, my mind continues to twist itself into a self-deprecating knot I fear will always linger in my mind. Even if I—we—get the girl, I bet I'll always feel like a failure. *Because I am*. I failed the girl I loved when she needed me.

I may not know what happened after we stopped

replying, but the trauma cues are there. How do I battle the past that seems to haunt her? Especially when I'm one of her demons.

"You'll never push that with so much on your mind." Levi's voice jolts me out of my thoughts and racking the bar in front of me. His smirk dies when I look at him. "What's wrong, man? You've been off all week."

It's true. Ever since our dinner/movie night last week, I've been antsy. Blue's been a bit distant since then, and it's making me anxious. *Is she regretting what we all did?*

"Nothing," I force out and actually look at the weight I added to the bar for the first time. Two hundred fifty pounds. I *can* do it, but my long arms will make it a bit harder.

"Blue giving you a run for your money, huh?"

Honestly, I had already forgotten Levi was standing by the bench. "Yep." I debate taking ten pounds off to be safe, but I need to feel some kind of fucking accomplishment this week.

"Leave it," Levi demands and moves around the back. Gesturing for me to take my position to bench press, he waits. "I'll spot. You focus."

"It's hard to fucking focus when everything I do is probably wrong," I snap.

Levi doesn't miss a beat. "When I first met Blue, she avoided any and all kinds of friendships. That woman was just getting through each day trying to give Violet the best one possible."

I cross my arms, feeling defensive and a little annoyed that Levi didn't take the bait. I'm itching for a fight which isn't like me. Goddamn it, she has me all bent out of shape.

He doesn't look at me when he's talking, instead focusing on a distant memory over my shoulder. "I thought her cool personality was alluring. We hooked up a few times—"

I stiffen and immediately start sweating like hellfire is about to leak from my glare and incinerate Levi on the fucking spot. "WHAT?!"

"Calm down. We never had sex." Levi waves me off like I didn't just learn that my friend had a sexual relationship with my woman. "She was the last woman I was with, and not because she was bad. Fuck she was *amazing*."

This son of a motherfucking—

"Blue challenged me. Asked me the questions I didn't know to ask myself about preferences...my sexuality. Blue became one of my best friends because she was a key person in my self-discovery. I love her. She's my family and the reason I'm married to Kevin."

There's a wistful look on Levi's face that I can't help but take into account. Plus, his words are thoughtful and all-encompassing of the woman Blue has grown into. In some sick way, considering my own feelings, I'm glad Levi had Blue to help him.

"What I'm trying to say..." Levi pulls me from the war that's raging in my head. "Blue spent so many years thinking about everyone else. *That* was her coping mechanism. Me, Janine, and the others all work so hard to encourage Blue to have her own voice."

"She would rather make everyone else happy..." I

ponder out loud, not enjoying how those words feel coming out of my mouth.

"Because then they won't leave," Levi finishes my statement with a heartbreaking truth I didn't even think of. "Roman, Blue is still learning how to be happy."

I frown thinking about all the great stuff she does and her new job. "I thought she was, though."

Levi gives me a sad smile. "She did too until you four wiggled your way into her life and showed her she could have *more*. But only if she accepts all the hurt in the past and moves on."

My forehead aches with the depth of my frown. I feel like Levi's talking in riddles, but maybe it all makes sense in a complicated, messy, beautiful way.

"Blue's figuring out how to allow *more* into her life. She grew up with less and built herself a life giving to others. She'll figure out that *taking* isn't a bad thing, and that she *is* worthy of love."

My heart cracks and bleeds. Of course I've thought of what wounds she may carry after her childhood and young adult years, but hearing someone else's observation who is much closer to her than I am right now is painful. It's sharp like an ice cube slicing down my throat, forcing me to process the chill and wait for it to be warm enough to digest.

The thing is, I don't think I'll ever be able to digest the death of Erica Bennett. But watching the evolution of Blue will be, without a doubt, the highlight of my life.

"Love the determined look," Levi interrupts my

epiphany like the ass he is. He points to the bench and bar. "Now lie down and give me three."

Amped up and ready to take on the world, I bench press two hundred fifty pounds two and a half times—Levi helped the last one—but you know what, that's *absolutely* a win.

Forty-Five

BLUE

"**M**ama...there's a reason I wanted us to drive separately."

Violet hasn't stopped glancing at me every few seconds for the past five minutes. I've been waiting her out, hoping like hell she'll finally open up about what's been going on.

The ups and downs have been jarring. Like the day after we had dinner with the guys and she ditched me in their home of sexiness, she was completely different again.

I had been hoping, since she was bright and bubbly again for a few days before today, that whatever happened had passed. Nope. I was wrong. I felt a bit out of sorts the next morning after Jared made me come. So I wasn't prepared for teenage angst again.

Violet actually refused eye contact all day and admitted she was having friend trouble. Pissed, I tried to ask her to elaborate, but she told me to back off and locked herself in her room the rest of the day. I've been left feeling like I have a sixteen-year-old who, unfortunately, has the privileges of an eighteen-year-old.

Once again, my nerves were shot to shit, and all I could seem to focus on is everything that could be wrong in my kid's life. Not to mention, I felt like shit for not knowing.

We're closer than mother and daughter, closer than cousins. We've been through some shit. For once, she's not allowing me to go through it with her.

"Why, V?" I ask softly, not wanting to spook her by sounding too manic. Pushing too hard would definitely push her further away. It feels like she's finally reaching for me, and I'd be a fool to mess it up.

I swear I hear Violet gulp. It's Halloween, our favorite holiday. The one we always bond on, but she feels so far away this year. Is this what being a parent is? The crippling sensation of something precious slipping through your fingers?

Violet invited Roman, Felix, Jared, and Declan to the theater with us, and while she didn't cancel on them, she begged to have them drive separately. I was a bit taken off guard, but of course I said yes. Honestly, I was thinking she might not want to be stuck in a car with four large men that I've kept in limbo since the summer.

"Violet?" *Don't push, don't force.* I'm fucking terrified, though.

She sighs far heavier than any teenager should, which makes me feel horrible. Like I've failed her. "So, don't be mad."

Fuck. I stiffen. We're three fucking minutes from the theater where the guys are already waiting. This feels big, and yet we have minimal alone time to actually talk.

"Okay..." I agree hesitantly. My ass is sweating.

"There's this guy...*person*...on my socials who won't leave me alone."

I tense, every protective mom instinct powering on and flipping right to fucking high. Immediately I start going through all the self-defense moves Violet doesn't know. *She's not safe.*

Violet continues while twisting her phone around in her hands. "I've blocked him. I block all the weirdos, but he keeps making new accounts and messaging me again."

Don't flip out. You're driving. Just keep driving. Let her talk.

"I know it's the same person because he always says the same things. It's weird. Sometimes he goes a few days without creating a new account, but he always comes back." Violet shivers, and I almost punch the steering wheel. *Who's harassing my kid?!*

The theater comes into view, and relief whooshes through me because now I can get out and scream without worrying about crashing the car. Simultaneously though, I feel trapped in the fact that there are four men waiting for us to go see a movie and there's no way Violet isn't going to rush in there to avoid a hard conversation.

Shit on sticks.

"I—I don't know what to do, Ma. I'm scared."

My throat closes over, and my eyes immediately burn. The sun has set, so the streetlights and outdoor signs blur and expand in my vision. "V..." I would like to ask her why she didn't tell me sooner, but that's not the right approach.

So what is the right approach?

I wish on everything I could ask myself *what would my mom do*, but I had nowhere near enough time with my mom to truly know her parenting style. The only thing I can think of is removing Violet from the situation.

Gulping, I turn into the parking lot. I keep driving until we're at the front of the theater and I can see all four of my men chatting just inside the doors.

"Blue?" Violet sounds worried.

With a deep breath, I unlock the doors and hold my hand out. "Unlock your phone and open the app, please. Then I want you to get out and walk right to Roman. Ask for a hug and have Declan order me an Icee. Tell Felix I'll be inside in a few minutes and need a girl moment. Give Jared a pointed look so he knows to stall Felix for me."

She looks at me with wide eyes even as her fingers unlock her phone with the precision of an eighteen-year-old. "And what are you going to do?"

I tuck her blonde hair behind her ear and smile as bright as I can all the while I'm trying to tamp down the violence attempting to pour from my veins. "I'm going to park, read the messages so I know what we're dealing with, then I'm going to figure out what we should do."

"We?"

At that, I really do smile. "We are always a *we*, Violet. Now go. Make sure the popcorn has butter and salt in the middle too."

She laughs and unbuckles her seatbelt. When Violet reaches for the handle, she pauses and looks back at me. "Thank you. I love you."

"Love you, baby girl," I whisper and grab the phone from her.

I watch her walk inside and right into Roman's embrace. He'll know how to manage her worries right now while I come up with a game plan. Declan will need a distraction, and sugar is best. Felix will worry, but Jared has always been able to talk everyone off the ledge.

I just need a few minutes.

Parked, I eye the bright screen of Violet's phone and take a heavy breath. No wonder she's been so down lately. I don't even know what this person's been saying, yet I'm shaking and anxious beyond belief.

Gathering courage, I open the first unknown thread. Bile rises. Then the next and the next until I'm so angry I barely remember to pull the key out of my ignition before exiting the goddamn car.

Who does this asshole think he is, demanding Violet's location over and over again?! The threats following each one become more and more gruesome with each new profile.

How dare *anyone* come after V this way?! Her mother may be a deadbeat, but this dick is acting like she doesn't have an army surrounding her.

I worked my ass off creating a group of loyalty, strength, and so much love the world would burn if ever wielded with aggression for *her*. My cousin. My kid. My fucking *daughter*.

I raised her. Blue Bennet. Nobody will *ever* touch a hair on her head. I don't care if it's *me* that takes the fall for whatever hell I'm going to rain down on this bastard, as long as she's safe.

While the heat nipping at my heels is filled with rage, my heart warms when I catch sight of Jared and Felix laughing with Violet who stays close to Roman. Declan's struggling with so many snacks I can't help but grin.

Crack!

My jaw explodes with so much pain and shock that my knees buckle. The only sound that comes from me is a wet squelch. Blood flies from my busted lips as I crash to the sidewalk.

Boom!

My eyebrow takes the brunt of my fall and yanks reality from right under me. Darkness swallows me, and yet...I'm not afraid. *I'm proud*.

I'm proud because I made her get out of the car. I'm proud I trusted my soul which told me Violet would be safe with Roman, protected by Felix, seen by Jared, and lightened by Declan.

My future looks dark now, but it's okay. It's okay because this found family I've created over the years and the apartment I worked so hard to pay off will take care of her. My reason for living. Not only surviving. I *lived* for Violet, and I did it right.

I'm leaving so much love and stability in my wake. That has been my only goal.

I'll go feeling proud and accomplished because my daughter will be safe and loved.

I'll go, and everything will be okay.

I'll go.

Wilted Duet

COMPLETE ON NOVEMBER 15TH, 2025

Petals of Blue
Part 2
~MMFMM
~Trauma
~Badass FMC
Pre-Order Here!

Also by Y. V. Larson

Always With You duet
(Completed)
A dark, emotional MMFMM romance
Never Moving On
Never Losing Hope

Wherever We Go series
A series of interconnected single mom MMMMF
standalones
Just You & Me
Simply You & Me
Utterly You & Me (TBD)

Collapse of the Premuim Designation series:

The Invisible Omega duet
A dark, emotional academy MMFMM Omegaverse
Met Your Match
Met Your Mate

The Torn Omega duet

A dark, post academy MMMFM Omegaverse

Who We Were

Who We Are

Perfidious Passion

A dark, emotional Valentine's Day Novella

Damaged duet

A dark, emotional MMFMM romance

Beyond Repair part 1

Beyond Repair part 2

Wilted duet

A dark, drama filled, emotional MMFMM romance

Petals of Blue part 1

Petals of Blue part 2 (November 2025)

Stalk Me!

Website

Facebook

Instagram

TikTok

Amazon

Acknowledgments

First and foremost, I need to say thank you to my husband for being my biggest cheerleader! When I started this journey a few years ago, I never would have thought I'd be here, yet he never once doubted me. Sometimes he has even been far more excited about my accomplishments than me! I'm so thankful for his support and encouragement.

When I first started writing, I was worried about how my friends and family would react to my genre of choice. All the people supporting me and cheering me on have pleasantly surprised me. Many of my family members have even read some of my work *blush*. Thank you to my parents and in-laws for not judging me or frowning at my work. It means the world to me that I can share my dream with the people I love the most.

My PA! Thank you Aubrey for managing all the things I don't understand and being patient with all of my questions! You're my rock!

ALPHAS! Angelica... Patricia... Brandi... Kassandra...you got me through some moments of uncertainty. The hype you ladies have given me has been beyond my wildest dreams! Your kind words and helpful critiques left me feeling proud of my work. Thank you from the bottom of my heart!

Scarlett, my editor! You are amazing. I have no idea how you do it, but I am in awe and so thankful for the effort and work you put into this story. Thank you!

Proof reader…Miss Erica — Who lived vicariously through Blue for her fun name! You're amazing and the talent you have is so appreciated!

S.E. Green, my book bestie! I feel like I need to say thank you for so many things. For everyone reading this, S.E. is literally everything. Thank you for keeping me sane, reading all my random snippets, calming me down when I get a bad review, being my cheerleader, teaching me all the techy things, etc. I could keep going! Thank you for being so amazing all the time.

READERS! You all blow my mind. Thank you for all the kind words you have given and for taking the time to allow my stories to take up a little portion of your day. I write what I love to read, and I'm so honored to have a space in your libraries.

About the Author

There are so many things I could say but none of the words would live up to the absolute wonderful chaos that is my life. I'm a mother. A wife and daughter. I'm a reader and a writer. I JUST completed my masters degree in marriage and family therapy too. One degree hotter!

I'm a woman who has never forgotten how often her twelve-year-old self dreamed of being an author. I've always said writing is my dream and mental health is my passion. I am motivated and blessed enough to peruse both while loving my family with my whole heart and soul.

The hard days are tough. The lows are pretty deep. And the highs... they are what I live for. Being everything that I am has come with challenges but wow are they beautiful ones.

The pages you'll read show emotion and despair because I am not only the roles I fill for others. I was a kid who felt loss and internal pain. That part of me is still in there begging to be seen and heard... so this is me... my trauma dump in dramatic form. My FMC's live horrible lives, and while their experiences are far beyond mine, their feelings are often my own.

I struggle and I cry. I feel worthless and sometimes

like I'm fighting every day just to be enough. Their stories are mine in a way. Please read with empathy as trauma responses are different for everyone.

My stories and yours are valid and worth being heard. Don't ever lose sight of the battles you've overcome.

And take care of yourself, please.

With appreciation and empathy,

Y.V. Larson